LAREE BAILEY PRESS
First Edition: APRIL 2016
ISBN: 9781630351038 (Paperback)
ISBN: 9781630351021 (eBooks)
ISBN: 9781630351816, 9781630351823 (Large Print)

STRIPPED 2

CHAPTER 1
CASSIE

With Jon's coat wrapped around my shoulders and the blanket draped over my hips, I watch the two women on stage. Their laughter rings true, and I can't help feeling envious. Their lives must be so much easier than mine. I haven't laughed myself sick for a very long time. A combination of tears and terror ward off any moments of pure bliss.

I feel Jon's gaze on the side of my face. He leans close so we're nearly cheek-to-cheek and whispers, "As far as I know, they both have a bag of demonic cats living in their brains. That chick," he nods at Sidney, "confronted my mother."

My jaw drops and I stare at him, gaping. "No." The word is drawn out, and my unspoken question hangs in the air—who has the balls to challenge Constance Ferro?

"Yes. That one," he points to Avery, "she's still fighting the tide, but refuses to go under."

"How do you know that?"

He shrugs. "I sense it." I suspect there's a story behind his comments, but Jon dodges further discussion by joining Trystan by the stage.

Trystan Scott—blue-eyed heartthrob, sex on a stick, and all around ladies man—pushes back into the dark leather chair, worry pinching the tanned skin between his eyebrows. Dark hair falls into his eyes as he claws the arm of his seat, backing away from the crazy chick making herself at home in his lap.

Sidney and Avery stand arm in arm in mirrored poses, their opposite hands on their hips. Avery calls out, "Hey, little bro Ferro." She laughs and says to Sidney, "He's not very little is he?"

Sidney shakes her head and giggles. "I've heard nothing about him is little."

Peter, who had been standing quietly behind me, is suddenly across the room and marching up the steps. "Hey!"

Sidney smiles at him as he crosses the stage and wraps her arms around his waist. "Girls like to talk, and it's hard to avoid hearing rumors since people ask me way too frequently about you."

Peter's eyes turn into beach balls, and he nearly chokes. "Excuse me? Where do people ask you these things?"

She shrugs, ticking off a list on her fingers. "At the market, at school, in the ladies room." She looks over at Avery. "Do they bug you about Sean?"

"They think I'm a hooker, so I'm invisible." Avery picks at a spot of glitter on her arm. "Besides, my profession doesn't exactly make me a credible source. Who cares if Sean's call girl said he's huge?"

Everyone stops and gawks at her. Bryan stops teasing Trystan to give his full attention to Avery. "He hired you?"

Stunned faces snap to hers, but Avery's expression remains placid as if she's accepted it and moved on. In the echoing silence, a needle could drop and sound like a grenade.

Jon practically growls, "I don't know why anyone is shocked. We are talking about Sean." He seems pissed, and shoots a quick glance at me from the corner of his eye, then moves across the room to sit by Trystan.

There's a sinking feeling in the pit of my stomach. Based on the facial expressions of the people here with me, I'd guess it's contagious—we all feel it.

I keep my eyes down, but I hate that Jon said it. I hate the way no one tries to protect her. Strength on the outside is just that—outside. It doesn't keep the world from trampling your heart.

I find my voice, "She's more than that, you know." The words spill out, and once I start I can't stop. I jump up, dropping the jacket and blanket behind me. I pad toward him, standing there covered in glitter, my corset hoisting my breasts to my throat and my thong revealing my entire backside.

Jon realizes how it sounded and attempts to correct, but he's already flown that thought into a mountainside. "I know, but—"

"No little girl says, 'I want to be a stripper when I grow up.' Not one of us would sell sex if there'd been another way to survive. Every single woman who works here has the same story—fucked up life, no money, and no hope. Don't you dare damn her for it! If you do, you're damning me, too, and I refuse to accept your pity, or whatever the hell this is." I'm in his face, an inch from his nose, breathing hard. It looks like I'm going to pop out of my corset every time I breathe. Mounds of flesh swell well above the low neckline, glittering like twin disco balls.

I expect him to look at me, but he doesn't. Jon presses his lips together, letting his silence build between us while the others stare in shock. When his blue gaze lifts to meet mine, he tips his head to the side. No trace of a smile softens his lips. Nothing subdues his sharp look. "You don't know Sean. He'd show up with a corpse if it suited him."

Something inside me snaps. I straighten, laughing bitterly. "You're an asshole."

"No, I'm not. I'm just saying—"

"Shut up, man. She hears exactly what you're saying." Trystan peers around the girl in his lap, forgetting his own awkward situation for the moment. The girl sits perfectly still, but I can see her thoughts running wild behind her eyes.

Jon growls, "No, she doesn't. This isn't about any of you. It's about my brother and me." There's obviously a huge rift between Jon and Sean, but he's poking a bear with Pixy Stix. What does he think is going to happen?

"It might also be about your apparent distaste for working girls." Avery folds her arms over her chest and juts one hip to the side, glaring at him. "So, Little Ferro, spill it. Did your first hooker mistreat you? Or was it one of your strippers?"

Jon's body tenses and he sits so still he might explode. It's the moment of utter silence before a bomb detonates and blasts everything around it to bits. One of his fingers presses into the chair, and I see something flash across his face. It's raw, a wound that's still weeping.

He's quiet for a moment, swallows hard, then stands and walks into the office. The door closes soundlessly behind him.

Something happened to him. I'm sure of that. Someone hurt him badly.

Apparently Avery senses it too because she slips off the edge of the stage and rushes toward me. "I'm sorry. I didn't know."

I glance at the closed door and then back to her pale face. "Neither did I. I'm not sure any of us did."

CHAPTER 2
JON

I feel like a fucking idiot walking away to hide in the office. I'm not a kid anymore. This shit shouldn't bother me, but it's always lurking—ready to rear its fuck-ugly face when I least expect it. Of course they all think I had hookers and strippers. I'm not a priest. I'm a Ferro. I live up to my reputation and then some. But that's not what made me back down. I know I don't see things accurately at times. I know my past taints my vision, clouds it, and makes me respond in the worst possible ways.

I sit down at the desk and stare at the packet of papers. I wonder if I'm reacting to Sean or my past. How can I protect Cass when I can't even deal with this?

There's a knock on my door, and before I can answer, Avery steps inside.

"Hey," she says, "I didn't mean to do that." She's standing there, her long brown hair sweeping over her shoulders and a somber expression on her face. She steps around the door, pushing it shut behind her with the heel of her foot. No shoes.

"You didn't do anything." I'm not telling her shit. She'll report back to Sean, and I don't want him involved in this. His chance to intercede is long gone.

I shuffle through the stack of papers on the desk, ignoring Sean's envelope. I'll look at it when she leaves.

"Maybe not, but it seemed like I found a sore spot and ripped it wide open."

I act like it doesn't matter. I'm not telling her shit. "I misspoke. Cassie is hurting. It was reasonable to assume I insulted all of you."

Avery stops in front of my desk, turns to a ninety-degree angle from me, and rests her denim-clad hip against it. She folds her arms loosely across her chest. "We're all hurting."

I glance up at her. Is that a hint? Is something going on with my brother? "Sean included?"

Her eyes dart to the side. She pushes off the desk and looks at a picture of the club on the wall. All the dancers are standing with the bouncers and the former owner, posing as if it were a yearbook picture. "You don't know him anymore, do you?"

"There's nothing about him that's worth knowing." I sound like a cold motherfucker, like I don't give a shit about my brother, but the tightening sensation in my chest tells me otherwise. The growing unease in my stomach, the way it twists like it's filled with shards of glass, reminds me of something I don't want to admit. I suppress it with one swift blow, forcing my emotions back down where they belong. "Maybe you don't know, so I'll tell you the drive-by version. Sean thinks I'm a piece of shit stuck to his shoe. No one willingly walks through shit, Avery. He's here to save his ass. It has nothing to do with me."

"You don't know him."

I appreciate the audacity of this woman. This is the first conversation we've had, beyond initial pleasantries, and she's picking a fight? I lean back in my chair and look at her. She's smart. I'd bet anything that she's scanning that picture for Cassie's face. It's not there. Cass always dodges pictures, probably because of her ex.

I roll my eyes and sit up quickly, reshuffling papers that don't need it. "I don't want to know him. There's nothing there worth saving, no way we'll ever be anything but blood. I don't give a shit what he does or if someone puts a bullet in his head. Actually, I've been waiting for it to happen. Between his past and the shitstorm in the press, it's only a matter of time. I wouldn't get too attached, Avery." It's a dick thing to say, but this conversation is over.

She takes the hint and heads to the door. Her hand rests on the knob for a second then she looks over her shoulder at me. "Too late. I'm already attached." She smiles sadly, watching me until I meet her eyes. "And no matter what you think, Sean cares about you. I see it in his eyes. I hear it in his voice when he talks about you. Think what you want, but take it from someone who knows what it's like to be utterly alone—Sean's here out of more than loyalty. You're more than blood to him. I'll see you around." She walks through the door without waiting for a reply.

CHAPTER 3
CASSIE

Trystan and Bryan are staring at me. I can't blame them. Up close, I look like a porn version of Tinker Bell. My cleavage glitters as I breathe, sitting silently on a stool, wishing I hadn't tossed the blanket and jacket on the floor. Picking it up feels like a betrayal, so I sit there half-naked with a rock star and a Ferro. Sidney and Peter left when Jon walked away.

The other girl watches me from Trystan's lap, her golden eyes boring into me. "Oh, holy fuck, girl! You're making them drool. Someone is going to step in that shit and slip. I don't wanna break my ass on a concrete floor, so you need to put on the fucking jacket." She's up across the room, sweeps Jon's jacket from the floor and tosses it at me. "Pride ain't got no place in here."

"My pride dried up a long time ago." I slip my arms into the sleeves one at a time and watch her sit down next to me.

"Bullshit. It's buried beneath the lies you told yourself to pull this kind of thing off. You're right, though—no one wants to do this shit. It gets chucked at you, and you gotta learn to play catch." She leans forward and rests her elbows on her knees before folding her hands together. They dangle between her knees as she stares at me. I feel like I'm about to get cracked open and fried on a hot skillet.

After a moment, as if she's judged me worthy, she holds out her hand toward me and says, "I'm Mel."

"Cassie," I say, loosely accepting her outstretched palm and allowing her to shake mine firmly.

Trystan is quiet, listening. No matter what the press says, he's not the womanizer I expected. His noticeable silence betrays his perceptiveness, always watching and listening. He soaks up the world around him, analyzing it, only speaking if he has something worth saying. Trystan doesn't talk to hear the sound of his voice.

Bryan on the other hand... I can't read that guy. He's sending out so much interference it's hard to tell what he truly thinks about anything. He's leaning back against a worn black leather club chair, one arm draped across the back, his fingers dangling over the edge. "You speak for all women everywhere, I'm sure." He grins, and I know he's provoking her on purpose, although I don't have a clue why.

"Hell, yeah, I do." Mel blasts back.

"And that explains why so many women enter the sex industry yearly. It has nothing to do with ambition, power, money, or control. It's all a sob story with no ulterior motives." Bryan smirks and looks up at Mel from under those dark lashes, his green eyes sparkling.

This guy wants us gone.

Sensing the tension growing thicker, I interrupt, "You're right. You nailed us. We're faking. We both came from good families with reliable parents to love us. The truth is..." I lean in close. Bryan is sitting across from me. He straightens in his chair, glances at Trystan, and then leans across to get closer to me. "I know you want us to leave, and you should have just said so instead of jabbing verbal shivs at us until this girl rips your face off. Dick move."

Bryan regards me oddly, and whispers, "There's a shitstorm coming. Get out of here and don't come back."

Mel stares at him.

I shake my head. "I have to come back."

"For work?"

I shake my head again. "For Jon. I'm not walking away again."

"You're the reason his life is a never-ending rave. It's a perpetual party to drown out the pain you caused him the last time he was fucking you. So, here's a tip—leave before I make you." Bryan is on his feet, glaring down at me.

I rise and feel all eyes on me, waiting to see what I'll do next. "I never slept with Jon. I know I hurt him. If I could undo it, I would. I was young and naïve, but I'm not anymore. I won't let anyone near him. No press. No nothing. The papers Sean gave him—is that his best move?"

"If he doesn't want his mother to bury him alive in the garden, yeah." Bryan sneers at me, clearly frustrated. "You have no idea what you've done here, what's going to happen to him because of this. You shot off your mouth about your chosen profession—we all know you chose this, ladies—and you got to him. Jon never backs down. He has rhino balls. He rips apart anyone threatening him or his family until you came along. We're not making the same mistakes twice. Walk away."

I suck in a jagged breath, wishing I could hide it, but I can't. "No. He didn't walk away because of me. Are you blind? Something happened to him."

Bryan gets in my face, looming above me with six feet of ass-kicking ability usually disguised by a grin. "It's not your concern. We've got this."

"Bullshit." I shake my head and ball up my hands into fists to try to contain the rage steaming inside me. I can't let it out. They'll write it off as PMS and nothing more. I level my voice, holding it steady, forming my words slowly, and enunciating each point. "If you had this, Jon wouldn't have bought this place. If you had this, he wouldn't have that old, festering scar. If you had this, he'd still be the guy I met that summer—the one filled with hope, not pain. You don't have this. You never did. You don't even know what 'this' is."

Bryan presses his lips together and fixes his eyes on Trystan. "You better show her the door before I do."

Trystan rises slowly and inhales. He lets out a rush of air and runs his hand through his hair. He glances at Bryan and then me. "May I talk to you?"

I feel his gaze on the side of my face, and I know he only wants to stop this from escalating. I'm not being a bitch. I'm worried about Jon. He's been behaving erratically, and none of his family seems to notice or care. I have no idea which, but I'm not walking away. Not today. Not ever.

I dig in my heels and glare at Trystan. "No. If you have something to say, say it here."

Trystan sighs. "Jon needs to sign those papers, and he needs to walk away from this." He gestures so that I know he's talking about the club. "He's refusing to hear anything we tell him."

"You're not my problem."

"Yes, but Jon is. If you care about him at all, you can't let him keep this place. Sean's a dick, but I believe he's genuinely looking out for Jon. Stuff happened between the two of them—I don't know what, it was before I met him—but that shouldn't be the reason his life now turns to shit." There's compassion in Trystan's eyes. "Listen, not too many people understand what makes Jon tick. It can get lonely, living like that, and I know he doesn't want to say goodbye to you yet. Talk to him. Make him see this is one of those times he's making life harder just to make it more difficult. He can help you without the club. You can help him by making him see that."

I look over at the woman silently sitting beside me. She makes a disgruntled noise and sinks back into her seat, slouching down in the chair and looking up at Trystan. "A fine brain to go with that fine body."

A slight blush rises to Trystan's cheeks, but he turns away so quickly I almost don't see it. A blushing rock star? How is that possible? Bryan misses it—he's too busy glaring at me.

My feral, pissed off stance relaxes, and I look away. Maybe he's right. It's possible this place will only bring Jon more pain, and I don't want that. His mother is demon spawn, and I won't be the reason he's in her crosshairs. "I'll get him to sign the papers."

CHAPTER 4
JON

Avery has steel balls coming in here, talking to me the way she did. This is my move, my decision. Sean has no fucking clue—no one does. They see what they want, and I learned a long time ago that you can't change the way people think of you. They see a foolish young guy who frivolously spends his cash on pussy.

If that's what they think, then so be it.

I pull my cell phone out of my pocket, dial her number, and press it to my ear. After the fourth ring, she picks up.

"Jonathan, I'm in a meeting. What do you want?"

Typical. My mother's maternal instincts are shit. Sometimes I wonder if we were all adopted. Since there are pictures of her pregnant, I have to believe we're biologically hers. Sean remembers Mom being pregnant with me and fussing over the nursery, while he and Pete beat the crap out each other. They fought a lot after I came along.

"I have news I thought you should hear first. I bought a strip club."

She's silent, probably pinching the bridge of her nose. I hear her excuse herself from the room, and then a door closes. Her voice is sharper than a kitchen knife as she verbally butchers me. "I'm out of patience with you Jon. I've explained what would happen if you were stupid enough to piss on the family name again. So tell me, dearest, why would you defy me so blatantly, and then call to flaunt your indiscretion in my face during a multimillion-dollar deal? Exactly what type of perverted asshole are you, son?"

I laugh bitterly and kick my feet up on the desk, happy for this to be over. "I'm the perverted asshole you raised me to be, Mom."

"Jonathan, I don't have time for your antics right now. It's been less than twenty-four hours, so destroy the deal and get your ass home. I'll deal with you later."

"No."

I've never said it to her like that before. It's clear, confident, and ringing with defiance. I normally laugh off whatever she says, and smile to her face. This isn't the type of fight we have. She yells at me, I laugh, and it gets shoved under the carpet. Not this time.

"I'm sorry," she hisses into the phone, "I couldn't possibly have heard you correctly, so I'll say it again and give you time to pull your head out of your ass, son. Get out of that property acquisition and come home. Now."

My jaw locks as every muscle in my body goes taut. "No. I'm not going back on a contract, not now, not ever. I'm not the man you think I am. I'm not coming home, and I'm not your fucking heir anymore. I'm my own man."

She laughs so shrilly my ears have that nails on a chalkboard reaction. I pull the phone away from my ear a little, but I still hear her scathing remarks. "You'll never be your own man because no matter what you do, you'll be walking under the shadow of your father. You aspired to be just like him, and that's what everyone sees—another manwhore with money. You're not the type of child a mother dreams of—you're the kind we dread. In the back of every parent's mind is the fear their child won't turn out right. What if he's too depraved to be a good man? What if he's a pathological liar, a narcissist, and likes the feel of blood on his hands? Congratulations, Jonathan, you've exceeded my worst fears for you on all accounts. Your inheritance is gone, and if you ever come here again, I'll make you wish you'd never been born."

I can barely breathe after that. I sit there stunned, staring at my boots long after the line goes dead. I whisper to myself, "You already did."

CHAPTER 5
CASSIE

When Avery exits Jon's office, she keeps her head down. At the last second, she glances up at me and offers a sad smile. I might suck at reading men, but that woman is an ally, a fighter, and a person who protects her own. She sees something in Sean that no one else does. I don't know if he hides it from them or if they're blind to it. The man probably puts on an act like the rest of us, but there's more to it than that. To have everyone who knows you think so poorly of you, it's odd—almost as if it were intentional. If everyone hates him, Sean has the space he needs to do whatever he needs to do with no one looking over his shoulder.

Avery walks past me then stops. She turns around. "Cassie?"

I turn toward her, stopping mid-step. "Yeah?"

"Thanks for saying something before. I try to act like it doesn't matter, but it's easy to tell it does when someone says something kind, protective. I'm not used to that. Thank you."

"I probably overreacted."

"Maybe, but if you hadn't, they wouldn't have listened. They all heard you. No one knows what's beneath the surface. You reminded him of that. I wanted to make sure I thanked you. It's rare for a stranger to put their neck out for me. Actually, the only other person I can think of is Sean. I'm glad I met you."

I can't help it, I smile. "Me, too."

She holds out her hand to me, and I shake it before she pulls me into a hug and slaps her hand on my back. She smells like strawberries. When she pulls away, she jabs her thumb back at the guys and says, "We know what they want, but I can't believe Jon doesn't know what he's doing. Maybe there's something else going on here?"

I know there is. Jon wouldn't have bought this place if he hadn't seen me the other night. I provoked him, and this is the repercussion. If Jon hated me, I could see him using the club to hold me here, but after that kiss, I know that's not it. I admit it. I have no clue what Jon's doing, what he's thinking, or why he's refusing to leave the club behind.

I part ways with Avery and pad over to Jon's door. I duck my head inside the office. "Jon?"

He has his feet up on the desk and a strange look on his face. He drops his boots to the floor and slips his cell phone into his pocket before glancing up at me and smiling softly. "Come in, Cass. You don't need to knock. Ever."

I'm holding my arms around my middle, clutching his coat to my body. I should be shivering, but I'm not. It's warm. I pull my arms out and hand it to him. Jon looks up at me and takes it. "Will you tell me something, if I ask?"

He nods without a second of hesitation. "Anything."

"Why not?"

He blinks at me even though he knows what I'm asking. Jon looks at the dingy carpet on the floor, avoiding my eyes, shutting me out.

"Jon, it seems like an arbitrary line in the sand. Why not sign the papers and live to fight another day?"

"Cass—"

"I'm serious. It's like you're trying to get disowned." As I say the last word, I realize what he's doing. I didn't see it until that moment. My brows wrinkle together as I ask, "Why?"

Still avoiding my gaze, Jon lifts the packet of papers and holds a lighter underneath. The little flame flicks to life, and he lowers the pages, his eyes focused on the tiny embers of paper as they ignite. "There's a reason."

"Is this the best way to do it? To walk away from them? From all of them?" My voice is too soft.

Jon bends at the waist to pick up an empty metal trashcan and tosses the papers inside. The dancing flames are reflected in his eyes. "Please don't try to bend the truth to make it easier to swallow. I know what they think, what they did. I'm going down in flames on purpose. They all expected me to. I'm just giving them what they want."

"You wouldn't have done this if it weren't for me."

"I would have done it before now, but it wouldn't have meant anything. Helping you changes everything. Club Ferro isn't going anywhere. They'll have to sue me to get the Ferro name off the sign, and they probably will. It won't surprise me if Sean torches the place tonight." His jaw locks as he speaks like he's lost in a nightmare while he's still awake.

I reach for him, place my hand on his arm. "Jon?"

When he looks up at me, there's pain in his eyes. Why haven't I seen it before? How could I not notice? I squeeze him gently and swallow hard, wondering what secrets are buried within this beautiful man that he wears a candy shell to keep people from finding out. His carefree airhead routine is an act—it always has been.

He forces a smile and squeezes my hand. "Cass, can I crash at your place tonight?"

My heart drops into my stomach. The way he looks at me, the way he touches me makes me think I should say no. I can't sleep with him. I can't even kiss him. Something's terribly wrong with him, and I don't want to be a rebound. I want to be his friend. He needs someone right now, and it's clear he believes he's alone, even though he's not.

Perception is reality.

"Of course," I nod. "I don't have a lot of room, though, and I need to make sure my roommate doesn't mind." His hand feels so good on mine, so warm and caring. I slip my fingers away while wishing I didn't have to.

"You live with someone?"

"Yeah, Beth. She's around here somewhere."

Jon smiles sheepishly. "I sent her home. I sent them all home—paid day off."

"Really?" I blink at him, shocked. "Why?"

"I didn't know how things would go with you, and I didn't want people around, so when you and I were in the pink room, Trystan brought them up to speed, paid them, and sent them home."

My jaw hangs open, and I stare at him. My mind is hung up on a thought, a small hook snagging me, bringing me back again and again. He thought something might happen, and if it were a fistfight, it'd be better to have people around. That's not it. Jon wasn't worried about me going batshit crazy on him. He wanted privacy—he wanted me. Here. Tonight.

My heart trips and stumbles inside my chest. I nearly choke and try to cover it up by coughing into my hand. I look everywhere except at Jon. My head is swimming in the smell of burning paper when I feel his warm touch on my arm.

Jon turns me around gently and releases my arm. Gazing into my eyes, he asks, "What's going on inside that head of yours, Cass?"

The touch makes me shiver, and my throat tightens. If I speak he'll hear it, he'll know how much I want him. It's not my fault. We've always been like this—attracted to each other beyond reason. And that's my issue, it's not what I want in my mind, but my body suddenly remembers it's in a corset, bound tightly. It makes my waist tiny and my breasts swell above the taut fabric. I'm wearing the wrong outfit for this conversation. Any physical reaction I have to him is obvious.

I laugh lightly, using the sound to clear my throat while trying to release the vice grip my hormones have on it. "Nothing. You surprised me."

Jon watches me as I try to avoid his gaze. I finally glance at him and shake my head. "What? Why are you looking at me like that?" His pondering gaze makes me antsy. He's not thinking about ripping my clothes off even if I am. There's something else there, something delicate—something raw—like a thread of hope on which he's hung every dream he's ever had. I'm scared it'll break. That he'll fall. That he'll turn into someone else.

Jon breathes in the smoky air and laughs. "I'm a man, Cass. You're wearing a corset. Don't ask me to explain how this works."

That's not what he was thinking about, but I act like it was. "I'll go change." I tap my fingers together and then pat my bodice.

"Yeah." He watches me too long, without blinking, thinking things I can't quite make out. He's tired and worried, but I get a glimpse of the Jon I met in Mississippi—young and vibrant, unafraid.

"Yeah." I echo his word, lost in thought, staring at his beautiful face. I wonder how differently things would have been for us if I'd never spoken to that reporter. We would have had our moment and burned up a long time ago. This wouldn't be here now, this chance.

The voice in the back of my mind reminds me I'm not the same person I was then.

It's okay. Neither is he.

CHAPTER 6
JON

Bryan has no fucking clue what I'm doing. He thinks I'm throwing everything away because of Cass, but that's not it. He doesn't understand. None of them do. Cass isn't the problem. She's my strength to do it—to walk away from billions of dollars, the cars, the mansion—everything.

As I lay on the floor next to her bed, I listen to the slow sound of her breathing, wondering if she's asleep. The apartment she and Beth share is abysmal. Below street level, with musty old carpet covering concrete, this space was designed to shelter stuff, not people. The ceilings are low, and there are no windows. The walls are the color of despair, and there's not much that makes this room Cassie's. No pictures, no frames of smiling faces, and nothing personal. Lingerie fills the tiny dresser, her pink corset set on top, with stockings hanging out of a drawer that won't close.

This room was meant to house the washer and dryer. The connections are taped off at the wall opposite me. I stare at the pipes and wonder how she lives like this. At the same time, she seems like she's surviving which is more than I've been doing. I've been buying time while slowly dying, waiting to be estranged from the woman who bore me. She thinks since she gave me life she can take it away. I wouldn't put it past her, but I need to break away anyway. My family is slowly killing me. One day I'll look in the mirror and the man I wanted to be will be too far gone to pull back from the abyss of shit I've stumbled into.

Cassie sighs softly and rolls over on the creaky bed. Her roommate seems to care sincerely about her. Beth didn't mind that I was here. Actually, a night off seemed to make her think more highly of me. Not many people do these days. By sunrise, I'll be lucky if my mother doesn't put a hit on me. Ferro family members are not disowned—they're annihilated, destroyed from within.

Sean will be the first in line when he finds out what I did. Bryan was pissed, but he has his own shit going on. Besides, when that guy gets high, everything is overly important to him. I don't know how many pills he popped tonight, but he was up there with the kites.

I never did much with drugs. I prefer being in control of myself. Since I lost

Cass, that's what I strive for—holding my shit together. I'm not letting anyone sway me. That's part of the reason I asked her if I could crash here. I want them to know I'm out of reach. The only question is how far will Mom go this time? I'm hoping I did enough to get shoved out, face-first, but not enough to get snuffed out.

Dad won't do shit if Mom decides one way or the other. He's too busy picking which pussy to feign interest in next. I don't want to think about him, or any of the mistresses. I don't want to remember what happened or what I did after that. Fucking my dad's lovers was twisted, but that's not why I did it. It was her. It all leads back to that point. I hate thinking about it. When the memories pop into my mind, I torch them with a blast of mental napalm, but nothing kills those fuckers. They spring back, ever vibrant, glowing—forcing me to relive it again and again.

I roll onto my side and face the metal frame of Cassie's bed. There's no fancy skirt on it, no storage boxes underneath. It's bare bones like the rest of her room— like the rest of her life. She said her husband dragged her back home once before. It's probably better not to own anything. Possessions make it difficult to disappear. With this amount of stuff, she could toss a change of clothes into a bag and become a ghost in less than five minutes.

The pit of my stomach goes into a freefall. Soft fingers sweep across my cheek and then gently drift away. I glance up and realize Cassie's head is resting on her pillow, which she's pulled near the edge of the worn out mattress. The springs sag in the middle. I can hear a corresponding squeak for every move she makes.

"Hey, Cass."

"Can't sleep?" Her voice sounds sluggish, and her eyelids are only half open. She hangs her arm off the bed and sweeps her fingers against my cheek again.

I grab hold of her for a moment, kissing the back of her hand to assure her I'm fine. "I'm okay. Go back to sleep."

She pats the bed and scoots back toward the wall. It's a twin mattress, and she didn't offer me that spot when she was awake. And now that I'm a little bit sleepy, and she's only half awake, I don't trust myself to use that place to rest.

"Come up here. I know you're tired, and the floor blows. Stop being a prude." She pats her hand firmly on the bed again, then hangs her face over the edge. "Don't make me come down there," Cassie says, yawning and blinking at me.

"I better not."

"We're both adults, Jon. I won't dry-hump your leg in the middle of the night."

"It is the middle of the night."

"Is that a request?"

I laugh lightly, considering it. Can I keep my dick to myself? Her scent is going to fill my head which will make it insanely hard in every aspect of the word. Before I have time to refuse, she grabs my wrist and pulls.

"Jonathan Ferro, come here." There's something about the way she says it that makes me move. I'm on my knees looking into her sleepy face and the tangle of dark hair around her cheeks. She sighs contently. "I know you need a friend. So do I. I promise I won't mess it up and neither will you."

"Tell me one friend you've slept with and I'll climb in next to you right now." She watches me and rests her hand on my face, her fingertips lightly touching my cheek.

"Trust yourself." She blinks slowly, sleepily.

"Do you trust me? I mean really trust that I won't do anything?"

"I trust you with my life, my heart, and my soul." She pats the bed again. "I don't want to sleep alone, and I'm betting you don't either."

I rise to slip into bed next to her, my heart thumping rapidly as all my blood heads to my boxers. I can't do this without wanting to nail her. No, it's more than that. I want to press my lips to her body, all of it. I want to learn every curve, taste every inch of her pale flesh. How am I supposed to hold her and not feel anything? She's going to notice. There's no way not to—the bed is too small.

"Cass, this isn't a good idea."

I don't notice until then, but there's a light sheen on her face, and it's not from sweat—it's from tears. She's been crying, lying up here alone. At that moment, the world shifts, and I don't care about me anymore. I pull her to me, pressing her face against my chest and holding her close.

With Cassie clinging to my chest and me squeezing her tight, time stops. I keep one arm wrapped tightly around her waist, firm and strong, while the other strokes her hair. I kiss her forehead a few times as I say things that are more sounds than real words. I don't ask her why she's weeping. I don't tell her not to cry. The truth is there's always something to mourn, but most of us don't take the time to do it. This will help her in the long run, so I let her sob softly on my chest until she falls asleep in my arms.

At one point she would have said this kind of intimacy was forbidden, reserved only for soulmates joined in marriage, and now that I'm here with her like this, I finally understand. Her slight form, breasts pressed against my stomach, her thigh draped over my leg, and the rhythmic sound of her breathing is a kind of physical closeness I've known before—it's the rest that's foreign. It's the way she doesn't care about the holes in her t-shirt, or that I can see the curve of her ass peeking out from beneath the hem. It's the way her hair is a mess, and she doesn't fuss with it or worry about the lack of makeup on her face. It's the way she doesn't hide her tears or her sorrow. It's the way she doesn't invent some story about being cold when I feel her nipples tighten against my chest. She doesn't hide anything from me. Cass is just there, being Cass, exposed. I see all of her because she lets me, because she invited me up here.

I close my eyes and breathe her in, committing every second of it to memory, knowing it'll never happen again. Tonight is a one-time thing. Cassie doesn't drop her guard even with friends, so this is rare. Even I know that. Tonight she came to me in the pink room ready to do anything I wanted. I can't reconcile the two women living inside of her. One is strong and daring, while the other is sweet and tender.

I kiss the top of her head and whisper, "I love you, Cass."

CHAPTER 7
CASSIE

I've been lying against Jon's chest with my eyes closed, trying to shut out everything else when I hear his voice. His faint whisper is raw, exposed, revealing something I'm not meant to hear.

"I love you, Cass."

It's hard not to react, to remain perfectly still in his arms. I manage, though, and after a while, I drift off. My usual nightmares give me a wide berth tonight. When I wake, he's still there, still holding me.

Something that feels too much like shame drips over me, coating me from head to toe. I look away and try to get up, but Jon takes hold of both my arms just below the shoulders, holding me in place and pulling me back down. I flop onto the pillow, looking straight into his eyes.

"I'm sorry." I say without giving it much thought, still trying to get away.

"If you get up again, I'm just going to pull you back down. Hey, look at me." Jon cups my cheeks in his hands, holding me so we're nose to nose. "What's wrong?"

I avoid his eyes. "Nothing. I just feel stupid. I shouldn't have asked you to do this."

"I'm glad you did."

There's too much silence. I glance up at him and instantly regret it. Dark lashes frame bright blue eyes on the most beautiful face I've ever seen. Jon has

always been stunning, but this morning he's radiant. I try to tear my gaze away, but the pull is too strong. He pins me in place, holding me in his gaze, saying so much without speaking a word.

Jon rubs his thumbs against my cheeks and my stomach swirls. Lust shoots through me, lighting every inch of me on fire. I want his hands on my bare skin, soothing this need, this ache to feel flesh on flesh.

Stop it, Cassie. Being with him will ruin everything. He said so himself. He doesn't want a married woman. I shouldn't want him either, but my body responds to his proximity without my permission.

My gaze drifts to his lips and the dark stubble surrounding his perfect mouth. I can imagine the scratch of him on my skin, the way that hot kiss would feel combined with the light scrape of his cheek. I'm lost in the past for a moment, remembered sensations overwhelming me—his lips on my wrist, his hand against my belly and

then lower. I gasp and jerk away, nearly falling on the floor.

Jon laughs and grabs me before I roll backward off the mattress and hit the floor. "You're insane! One moment you let me in and the next you're trying to act like I don't bother you."

"You don't bother me."

The corner of his mouth pulls up on the right side, revealing a dimple that rarely shows. "I make you hot and bothered. You don't have to admit it, I know. I always have." He grins seductively, and I can see how much he wants me. At the same time, there's kindness in his eyes, compassion for something he doesn't understand, something I'm not ready to explain to him. "Talk to me, Cass."

I don't want to talk. I don't want to tell him. I hedge, avoiding the question by leaning in and closing the distance between us. My heart beats faster as my lips start to tingle. I brush my mouth to his lightly, gently and close my eyes. The

excited rush of pleasure hasn't been there for a long time, but it's there with him. Still, fear pulses through me mingling with desire. I want more. With Jon, I always want more. Breathless I pull away, gasping. I sit up quickly and cover my mouth like I did something deplorable.

His hand is on my shoulder, but I shake it off.

"I can't." I can't kiss him. I can't be with him. There's no way to do it and not have him notice how fucked up I've become. The Cassie Hale he knew is gone, replaced by this woman whose veins run with fear instead of blood. Once in a while, I feel like I can break free and try, but to what end? I can't follow through, so why does it matter? It doesn't matter how I feel, at the end of the day the reality is always the same.

"You don't have to do anything. Cassie, please don't shut me out. Tell me what's going through your mind. I want to know.

I want to be here for you. Please." It's the last word, the plea that undoes me.

My reaction is primal—a defensive mechanism too practiced to stop. My walls shoot up, and before he can blink, I'm cold again.

"Cassie?"

Emotionally disconnect from that kiss, I tell myself, disconnect from him. My heart slows and the heat flushing my body fades. I stand and head to the small dresser for a pair of jeans and a t-shirt.

I'm on autopilot.

I can't stop it now.

I wish I could.

CHAPTER 8
JON

I don't press her for details. I act like nothing happened, like she's fine even though I know she isn't. Something spooked her. I want to fix it. The need to take her in my arms and hold her tight is overwhelming, but right now she'd fight me on it. She won't need me again until she falls apart. I have no idea how long that could take, and on some level I detest it.

There are too many parallels to the way things were before Cassie, commonalities with the way the bitch treated me. I never knew when that woman was coming or what she wanted. She just showed up and took it. Fuck. I rub my hands over my face and stop thinking about it.

I shower and wish I had time to jerk off. I'm so fucking tense it would help—but I don't. The water turns cold, and I'm out before I get anywhere.

The apartment is a deathtrap in the middle of one of the worst neighborhoods on Long Island. I wonder if I could get her out of here. I don't like this for her. It's not safe, but I doubt she'll let me help her.

I step out of the tiny bathroom with a towel wrapped around my waist. My hair is dripping a little, so I press my hands to my head and feel the water roll off my head and down my back.

"Wow."

I turn to see a woman, not more than twenty-five, sitting with her mouth hanging open. There's a piece of bread stuck to her lip and half an English muffin in her frozen hand. She's staring, her eyes glued to my chest.

I smirk and point between us with two fingers, gesturing between my chest and her eyes. "My face is up here, babe."

She gawks and finally remembers to blink. "Holy shit, you're fucking hot!"

"Yeah, I get that a lot."

"So do I, but damn." She ogles me, staring, and talking to my abs. "I could take that six pack out, drink it up, and marry it."

"Beth, cut it out. You can't stand it when guys do that to you." Cassie pads into the room wearing jeans, a tight white t-shirt and a pair of mismatched socks on her feet. Her hair is still damp from the shower.

"I wouldn't mind it from him. Damn!" She doesn't look away. Her tongue is hanging out of her mouth, and I'm starting to think she might try and lick me.

"Jon! Put some clothes on before there's an accident." Cassie grabs a cup and pours something dark from the coffee pot on the stove. She smirks at me from behind her cup. "You're going to kill Beth with sexiness."

"It's the best way to go," Beth mutters, swatting a hand at me. "Let him stay like this. No, wait! Tell him to drop the towel." She grins and slowly turns her head in my direction.

"Dork. Stop drooling over my friend." Cassie laughs and shoves Beth a little.

"I need a friend like him. Hey, Ferro, you can be my friend whenever you want." Beth winks at me.

I duck my head and rub my hand over the back of my neck while they talk about me. When I can get a word in, I point at Cass. "I'm going to get dressed, and then I'm taking you to breakfast, Miss Hale. Don't you dare eat a thing!"

STRIPPED 2

As I shut the door to the closet-sized bedroom, I hear Beth whisper, "You should eat him."

CHAPTER 9
CASSIE

As I emerge from the basement apartment, I blink at the bright sun and sneeze.

"Bless you, Cassie." Kam stands there, hand up, ready to thump on my head. He looks sheepish, lowers his floating fist, and pockets it. "Sorry, I wasn't going to knock on your face."

"No, of course not." I try not to laugh. For such a big guy, he's acting adorably bashful.

Kam's wearing dark cargo pants with a tight-fitting light gray t-shirt. It hugs his chest revealing every muscle the man has—and he's got a few. Okay, he has a lot. My first impression wasn't overly observant. I wasn't breathing right and didn't notice the way his oblique muscles tighten around his ribs when he moves. I can practically see muscle definition through his shirt.

Kam turns and walks up the steps, talking over his shoulder as he goes. "Yours is a pretty face, by the way."

I don't know what to say. Guys have said this kind of thing to me before, and it usually means they need something. "What do you want, Kam? I'm headed out."

He feigns hurt, pressing his hands to his chest and staggering back a few feet. Beaming that bright smile at me, he says, "Nothing at all. I thought you might want—

" His words die in his mouth when a head of dark brown hair appears in the bottom of the stairwell.

Jon bounds up the steps, talking without realizing Kam is standing there. "We need to find you a better apartment, Cass. You picked the worst possible street in the worst possible neighborhood." He blinks rapidly, focusing on the other man.

"Jon, this is my neighbor, Kam—" I step back to introduce them but am frosted over.

"I know. Kam O'Brian, Irish mob."

I glance at his dark skin and blurt out, "Irish?"

"I could be Irish," Kam says. "It's not an island of only white people with red hair, you know."

Jon laughs.

Kam shrugs. "Fine, I was adopted by a loving family."

"Yeah, don't let that fool you. This guy is just as Irish as the rest of them, adopted or not." Jon stares at Kam like he might kill the man. "So, why do you have a house in the 'hood, Kam? Need a place to torture victims where screaming is part of the background noise? Can't rip off fingernails in Dix Hills? The neighbors might talk, and then what would we do?" Jon's arms fold over his chest while he's talking. His shoulders square and his feet spread a shoulder's width apart, his whole body preparing to fight.

Kam remains calm, maintaining his less guarded stance. He strokes the hair on his chin, pinching the short chin rug between his pointer and thumb. "Exactly, Ferro. What would WE do? You've got just as much blood on your hands as us. No need to play dumb with me. I know that shit in the papers is a smoke screen."

"You think they pegged me wrong?" Jon sounds amused.

Kam nods, tucks his hands in his pockets, and swaggers toward Jon. "I do, and it gives you an unfair advantage. People think you're soft, stupid. They don't see the wolf hiding beneath the surface, ready to rip them a new one. Underestimating the enemy kills people, and I'm not losing none of my guys to a pasty freak like you."

Jon's lips slowly pull into a smile that covers his entire face. Chin tucked, he glances up at the guy. "Thanks for the compliment. I'm not here for you or your men."

Kam looks at me, then back at Jon, his eyes widening. "Is she your bitch?"

"Hey!" I snap and lightly kick Kam in the shin, still acting like he's my neighbor and not some nut job mobster.

Jon's eyebrows bunch together like I shouldn't have done that, but Kam hops back, a smile pulling at his mouth.

"Sorry, Cassie. I thought you'd own the fierce bitch persona. My apologies." Kam bows to me, then turns back toward Jon. "Is she your girl?"

"Cut it out, jackass," I say, commanding his attention. "Only call me a bitch when

I'm acting like one. If you two are finished peeing all over the place, I'd like to eat breakfast."

Kam slips his hands behind his back and suppresses a smile. "Awh-righ'," his accent thickens, and he kicks the grass beneath his boot before looking up at me. "No need to tell me twice." His tone drops an octave and the smile fades. He walks straight up to Jon and speaks in a lethal voice. It's so quiet I can't make anything out, except that he's clearly threatening.

By the end, Kam is nose to nose with Jon, grinning. "Don't test me, Ferro."

"Never give me a reason to, Kam."

"Then we have an accord?"

Jon makes a face. "Who the fuck talks like that? Yes, we have an agreement. You stay on your side of the street, and I'll stay on mine."

*****

Jon drives down the parkway at twice the legal speed limit. The engine purrs as he slams the gearshift up and down, bobbing and weaving between cars. I've nearly peed myself twice. I keep reaching for the oh-shit-strap, but there isn't one. Maybe rich passengers don't scream and cling to a leather strap when the driver accelerates too fast.

I'm trying not to shriek. Or curl into a ball on the seat. "Can we slow down?"

He looks over at me and wrinkles his forehead like it's a ludicrous suggestion. "Why?" He revs the engine as we duck between two cars with only a hair of clearance on my side.

"I'm going to puke. That's the main reason. The second reason is I don't want to die today. Why are you going all Speed Racer on me?" Jon's always been an aggressive driver, but I've never seen him like this. He seems to be sinking into his thoughts and merging mentalities with the car.

"Sorry," he slows a little and stays in a straight line for longer stretches of road than before. His lane changes are less abrupt now. "I don't like Kam being that close to you."

"How do you know him?"

He shrugs. "How do I know anyone? Alliances, family, connections, and money. Kam handles the dealers from here to D.C. He's the one who makes them fall in line or deal with the consequences. He doesn't live in that house, and you should never go in there. If you'd wandered in looking for him, his men would have killed you."

"I didn't. And I'm alive. Besides, I'd never roam around his house uninvited or even go out with some random guy."

Jon glances at me, confusion pinching his face. "He's not some random guy—you know him. At least, it sounded like you did."

"I do a little bit. I still wouldn't go anywhere with him."

Jon pulls off the parkway and merges into more traffic. His knuckles are turning white as he strangles the wheel. "Why not?"

"I don't know. I just wouldn't." I don't see it coming. Jon pulls over, stops the car, and flicks his hazard lights on. "What are you doing?"

"How many guys have you gone out with since we broke up?"

"What?" I roll my eyes. "What kind of question is that?"

"Answer me, Cass. How many?"

"It doesn't matter." I fold my arms across my chest and refuse to look at him.

"How many?"

"Less than you."

"That's not an answer."

"That's not a question! What do you want to know? Did I fuck the guys I stripped for? Did I take a few lap dances too far? Did I—"

He cuts me off, "Did you go out with a guy on a regular date after we broke up?"

I ignore the ominous pounding of my heart. This is only one shoe falling. The other will drop and kick my ass. I stiffen in the seat. "Yes."

"Was it Mark?"

"Yes."

"Did you go anywhere with any guy alone again after that?"

I feel sick. A jittering sensation builds in my gut, working its way into my stomach, and trying to come out of my mouth. I lock my jaw and stare straight ahead. I can't tell him what he wants to know.

"What did he do to you, Cass?" Jon's voice is a caress. His hand is about to touch my face, but I snatch it and jerk it away. Jon doesn't let go. "You can't tell me, can you?"

My eyes are glassy as memories collide inside my skull. Pulse pounding, I try to swallow, but my mouth has gone dry. I reach for the handle, ready to throw open the door and run, but Jon's grip on me loosens and slips away.

I remain in my seat, rigid, frozen with a fear of memories that feel more like nightmares. The corners of my mouth twitch as I try to hold the fake smile on my face.

I feel dead inside, and before I know what I'm saying, I'm answering his original question. "None. I'm never alone with men. Ever. I avoid it. You're my exception."

"Why?"

I glance at him. My eyes sweep his beautiful face and drink in clearly evident concern. His pink lips part in shock. I expected him to want to bury the man who did this to me, but he doesn't focus on that right now. His full attention is on me, and I know he's wishing he could erase the past. I know because I recognize that look. I've seen it too many times on my face in the mirror.

I press my lips together and try to put what I'm feeling into words. Something about confidences and trust. He never used me, but that's not it. It's not what Jon didn't do. It's what he did do. The man wanted me from day one, but he went at my pace and never made me feel like I had to do more.

Jon waited for me.

Mark was a monster in comparison. My thoughts are dark, so laced with anguish and regret I fight to force them below the surface. But here they are, displayed in the daylight, making me sick to my stomach. A shiver coats my skin, kissing me with cold that has nothing to do with the temperature. It works its way past the surface and slivers into my heart.

"You were the only one who didn't..." I can't say it. The words don't come. I press my fingers to my eyes and look down.

I feel Jon watching me for a long time before turning back to the windshield and staring down the street. Car horns blare around us as my head fills with the sound of Jon's breathing. I'm so tense, so nauseated, I almost miss it. I almost don't hear him.

His voice is barely a breath, a soft acknowledgment, "I know what you mean."

He glares at the road with hatred on his face. His knuckles are white as he clutches the steering wheel with one hand and the gear shift with the other.

CHAPTER 10
JON

Fuck, I almost said it. I nearly told her everything. Why would I do that to her? She'll never talk to me again if she knows everything. I can't lose her, not now. After all of this, when she's finally starting to trust me, why the hell would I even consider it?

I glance at her from the corner of my eyes. "Cass?"

She says, "Mmmm?"

I want to tell her. I want her to know everything about me and accept me the way I am. I accept her. I understand what she's talking about even though I wish I didn't. That fucker ruined her the same way the bitch ruined me. I can't be with a woman if it's anything but a good, hard fuck. The thought of letting my guard drop and letting her in—I can't do it. She'll find the scars, see the marks, and know.

Besides, it'll only cause her more pain, and I don't want that. I'm attracted to Cass, any idiot could see that, but I can't ever be with her. I can't fuck her. It'll never just be sex with her, and she's so defensive, so afraid. She's frozen me out again. Her replies are short, cold. I try to get my Cassie back, with the warm, sexy smiles, the girl in the sundress who thinks sex is affection at its core, but she's gone right now.

It's okay. She'll come back to me and next time, I'll get it right, and she won't run. I won't lie to her. I won't hurt her. I won't fuck her. I'll keep my hands and my dick to myself. If I love her at all, I know what I have to do.

Cassie glances over at me. I see the massive golden arches down the street. She still has no idea where we're going. It's two o'clock in the afternoon, and I promised the woman breakfast. Thank God for all day menus.

As I pull into the parking lot, I ask, "What would you like?"

She snorts and bows her head, hiding a light blush. "I remember the last morning we had McDonald's."

"So do I. I bought you everything on the menu."

"Jon?" Her voice is weak, near trembling.

I glance over at her. "It's okay, Cass. It'll always be okay with us. You don't have to say anything."

She looks relieved and settles back into her seat with a soft smile on her face. Cassie, my Cassie is still there. She's all soft curves and grace with a killer sense of humor and a sharp wit, but that's not what drew me to her in the first place. It wasn't her morality, although that piqued my interest, it was her conviction—the dedication she had to follow her beliefs. I didn't believe in anything then, never mind having the guts to act on it. Cassie has an internal compass that might be shattered, but it's not broken. I'll find my way back to her heart. I'll be there for her until she realizes I'm never leaving her side again.

CHAPTER 11
CASSIE

The other shoe never drops. Jon is there day and night, giving me space when I want it, and crawling into bed next to me when I ask. I feel bad about it, imagining him waiting around for something I can't give him. He wants sex. I know how to fuck. God knows I learned that lesson a long time ago. Emotional distance is a requirement of survival. At one point, Jon would have been all too happy to jump on that whore bandwagon, but not so much anymore. One night we stayed late at the club, and I told him I wanted to show him my gratitude. I made an ass out of myself, and he shot me down.

The next day I told him I needed to work again. I couldn't keep taking his money for doing nothing. As it is, I tried to give back the amount he'd paid me, but he wouldn't take it. The cash kept appearing in my apartment, in my jeans, or under my pillow.

When I told him I wanted to start stripping again, it looked like I sucker punched him below the belt. Jon didn't protest, though. He gave me my old hours back and a slot in the pink room. It was what I wanted. I was ready to fight for it, and I didn't have to. I felt deflated after that. I worked, silently noticing the same men every night. They ordered lap dances and over-tipped. While wondering why Jon didn't castrate them on their way out, I realized something.

Jon never watches.

He's not on the floor when I work, and nowhere near the pink room. At first, I was grateful to avoid the awkwardness, but then I noticed he's not there even in passing.

I wondered if I'd broken whatever we had, but decided not to dwell on it. For now, I just need to keep surviving.

In the dressing area, I pull off my sweatpants and sit there on the yellowed wooden bench in a light pink t-shirt, not wanting to get dressed yet.

Gretchen is cooing in front of her mirror, pursing her lips and grinning. She's wearing a glittery black pushup bra and G-string, thigh-highs, and shiny black heels. I'm barely listening until I hear his name. Gretchen arches her back and tosses her hair, laughing with a deep chuckle. "Who'd think Jonny would ask for me so many times, but he does. Private pink room party for two."

I glance at her. "Jonny who?"

The other women in the room quickly look away—except Beth, whose eyes dart between us. She stops dressing and becomes deadly still, her hands on her knees, waiting.

Ruby lips curve into an evil grin as Gretchen rises from her bench, clicking her way across the room toward me in her fuck-me heels. She leans in front of my mirror and preens, adjusting her amazing rack, then straightens to look down at me like she's so much better.

"Ferro. Who else would it be? What's the matter, Princess? Did you think he only liked looking at you?"

Beth sees me snap and lunges forward to stop me, but she's not fast enough. My hand pulls back and, by the time she does, it's too late. My fist is already flying headlong into Gretchen's face. I catch her cheek with my knuckles. The impact sends the dancer flying backward, and she falls to the floor. I don't stop. I can't stop.

I learned how to take a hit, and I learned how to throw one. Gretchen screams childishly and covers her face, trying to kick me off. "His dick is so big no one can satisfy him. It's not your fault, honey. He just needed someone better."

If she'd shut up for two seconds, I could regain my control. Instead, she elaborates, describing how she's sucked Jon off every night for the past two weeks. I should be crying, but my rage scalds any tears left to fall.

I'm on the floor, about to bitchslap her, when she drops her hand to taunt me. I have a clear shot at her face, and the girls around me are chanting, begging me to kick her ass. The background sounds dim to a forgettable buzzing, allowing me to focus on her claims of sucking Jon's cock. I imagine myself pummeling the bitch, and I know I can make her bleed. I know I shouldn't, but I can't stop myself.

I'm screaming at her, blasting her with words that make no sense, threatening her with things I'd never do. My hand is open as I swing my arm, intending to smack the arrogant expression off her face, but someone grabs my wrist and jerks me backward.

"What the hell are you doing?" Jon barely touches me. One swift movement pulls me away from Gretchen and to my feet, then he drops my wrist and steps back.

He's wearing jeans, no shoes, and no shirt. His bare chest is chiseled and glistening like he'd been working hard. He looks at me like I'm completely broken, attacking that woman without reason.

We're both fired. That's the old rules. Jon hasn't said much about them since he bought the club and plastered his name to the front of it. His mother has been freakishly silent as well. I know it's unnerving Jon, and he has better things to do than deal with this, but I can't help it.

"Don't touch me!"

Jon takes another step back and holds his hands up, indicating he won't. He's breathing hard, and his face flushes. "We can't have this shit in here. You know the rules, Cassie."

I'm breathing so hard my lungs feel like they are on fire. There isn't enough air. Bruce is there, scraping Gretchen off the floor, and shoving her belongings into a bag. She's pulling at his arm, trying to stop him, but the man might as well be a tank. "You know the rules. You're out."

Gretchen turns to Jon, eyes wide, full of tears. "Jonny, don't throw us out. Please."

Jon is glaring at me. He turns to her for a moment—we both do. "Why the fuck not?"

Bruce freezes, and there's not a sound in the room except Gretchen sniffling.

"We were just letting off some steam. Club Ferro is the best job I've ever had, please. It won't happen again. Things have been different since you came. I don't want to leave." She sways her hips, making it hard not to look at the G-string covering nothing. She approaches Jon, and he doesn't shut her down. He doesn't step away or anything. She touches his shoulder carefully, gently stroking his skin with her fingers. "I'll make it up to you, enough for this whole thing. For both of us."

Jon looks like Sean. He's stone, devoid of emotion, and I hate it. He lets her hang on him, making promises to suck him off for my sins too.

Screw that. I shove her out of the way and smack both palms into his chest. "No fucking the staff, huh, Ferro? What happened to that rule?"

"I'm not screwing anyone." His voice is cold, lifeless.

I hit him again shoving both hands hard against his chest. Is he with her? I can't process the thought. It gets stuck in my mind, gagging me, swirling around me and making me sick.

How could he choose her? I need to get a hold of myself. The little voice in the back of my head is telling me to get a grip, but I'm hysterical again. The veins in my neck pop up as my jaw tightens. I bite out the words and shove him as I say them, "Getting a blowjob is fucking!"

"Not here." Jon disregards me and turns away. He refuses to explain himself. It sounds like he's saying getting head is okay, and it's not fucking at all. I hear his voice from years ago—that young arrogant boy standing in the mall, telling me sex is a game, something to master. Meanwhile, I said it was about love and adoration.

In reality, sex is neither.

Sex is power over another human being. It's not fun. It's not sweet. It's a part of my past I wish I could erase. I still feel Mark's hands on the sides of my head forcing my mouth over his hard shaft, pushing too far into my throat, gagging me. Tears streaked down my face then, my ears ringing as he yelled at me, slapping the sides of my head as he ordered me to do it right, swallow harder, and suck him off.

Thinking about Jon doing that to someone kills me.

It's not the same, Cassie. Reason tries to call out to me, but it's no more than a distant echo that no longer holds meaning.

The same thought replays in my mind, like a CD skipping on a scratch.

Not Jon. Not Jon. Not Jon.

I'm too livid to form words. My entire body shakes, and I swear to God my skin will crack and explode. Growling, I race at him and jump on his back. I scream at him, "You're an asshole! A big stupid asshole who can't control his cock!"

Jon peels me off without effort. He holds my wrists above my head and twists my arm behind my back in a way that makes me move with him or get my arm broken. He shoves me back a few paces until my back hits the wall. Jon plasters his body to mine, pressing me into the wall with his bare chest, and holding me in place with his hips.

I try to twist out of his grip, but I can't move. My heart beats harder as an icy tendril of fear reaches up from within me. It weaves its way from my stomach, up over my ribs—making every muscle tighten—as it climbs to my throat and wraps around like a sleeping snake. I jerk my head back and forth, trying to kick free, but he won't move.

Jon hisses in my ear, "I'm not doing this here. You're losing it, Cassie."

His hot breath pours over my neck. I don't stop struggling. "You don't own me."

"I know that." His voice is too light. It registers that he's not yelling, that this isn't a fight. It's me.

I snap, "I can pay my way."

"I know that, too." He stops pressing on me so hard, and I can breathe again. Jon's eyes meet mine and lock. Sadness is buried so deeply within them, that I wonder if he even knows it's there. Pity clings to the corners of his mouth, and I don't want to hear those words. His lips part to say something, but I cut him off.

"I'm not the same girl you met in Mississippi, so stop staring at me like that. I grew up. So did you."

"Cass..."

"Don't treat me differently."

"I'm not."

"Yes, you are!" I try to shove him off, ignoring the tightening sensation in my throat. He's too big. I can't make him stop. I can't...

"Cassie," he breathes my name, begging me to stop but I can't.

I growl and thrash, screaming, "I'm the same as everyone else here! Stop acting like I'm not! I'm not different, so don't treat me like I am."

"That's not going to happen."

"Why?"

He hisses in my face, "Because you are different, Cass! Fucking get that through your head." He steps away abruptly causing me to fall forward. I stagger and catch myself.

I watch him retreat. His shoulders are tight, and his hands fist at his sides. He storms away, saying, "Fine, you're the same as everyone else here. Get your ass on stage in five or you're fired." His voice is detached like he doesn't care about me, but when he turns away, the scars on his back tell a different story.

CHAPTER 12
JON

Cassie is driving me fucking crazy. She lost her mind and went ape shit on another dancer. I can't take all this estrogen. That blonde, Gretchen, has been coming onto me every chance she gets. I nearly broke last night. She was naked, on her knees and pulling at my zipper, offering to suck my dick and swallow. Most girls catch on, but this one wants to be different. Her tits are tanned and huge. She shoved them in my face when I said no, then shimmied down, pressing them against my chest and slinked towards my hips where she kneeled and went for my fly. She got the button undone and the zipper down. She was about to touch me, to send me reeling with ecstasy when the unthinkable happened.

I said no.

I stepped away and zipped up. I refused head. What the fuck is wrong with me? I needed this. I'm Cass's friend. I can't fuck her even if I want to, so why say no to the blonde? Why send away those tits and that ass when it was so ready to be taken?

At one time, that would have never happened. At one time, I would have fucked her face, then tossed her on my desk and plowed into her until she shattered while screaming my name. I could take her high and leave her walking funny for a week. Refusing pussy isn't me. Yet, that's exactly what I did.

I sit in the grimy office behind my desk and run my hands over my face. Who the hell am I and how did I get here? My life is a goddamned mess. I don't even know who I am anymore. I'm surrounded by naked women every day, but I don't care. It's like they're not here. I used to get hard coming to clubs like this. My cock strained against my pants, and I was ready to take care of it, to nail any girl I wanted. They always said yes. Every single one.

Except Cassie.

And now I can't have her. That fuck messed her up so bad I can barely touch her. I should be grateful for what I have, but it kills me to see her flinch when I reach to stroke her face or take her bag. She acts like a kicked cat, skittish to the core. That's only the Cassie that's on the surface. The woman I knew is still in there, buried under a shitload of pain. Once in a while, I see it in her smile and hope floods my chest like a goddamned moron. Within seconds, she vanishes and days go by without touching her at all. She spooks and asks me to give her space, to sleep on the floor, to not touch her. When she showed up one day offering to screw me, I nearly lost it. She's hot and cold, and I know why. I get it. Shoving her into the wall was a mistake. It probably conjured memories of that sick fuck and that's the last thing I wanted.

Elbows on my desk, I hang my head between my shoulders and lace my fingers together behind my neck. I wish I knew how to free her. She's standing right in front of me, trapped. The chains aren't visible, but they're there. I don't know what to do. I can't treat her the same as the others. She's not the same and never will be.

I love her.

But that's not enough, so I tell her to stop screwing around and go strip.

I grab the hair at the nape of my neck and groan. I didn't want this for her. I can't change her. I can't fix it and make her better. The scars she bears will always be there, and they're much deeper than anything I've got.

The lie burns in my mind. That's not true. There's one scar, one thing still festering inside of me. I don't know how to deal with it, so I act like it's not there. That woman poisoned me and every relationship I'll ever have. There's a noose around my neck, and she can yank it whenever she wants to string me up.

"Fuck," I mutter to myself. When I look up, Trystan is standing there. He's got that look on his face—the one that says serious shit is about to drop. "What's wrong?"

He blinks rapidly and steps toward the desk with a blank look on his face. His lips part like he wants to say something. Day old ripped jeans and that leather jacket he's always wearing look wrinkled like he slept in his clothes. Trystan sits down hard on a club chair across from the desk. He stares at his shitkickers for a long time before finally meeting my eyes.

"Too much to fathom. But the main issue at the moment is there's some dick causing problems on the floor."

CHAPTER 13
CASSIE

My puffy eyes sting from crying. I wish I could rub them, but my makeup will smear all over my face. I focus my thoughts on the spotlight shining down on me and the pole in front of me. I'm on the center stage. Beth is to my right and a new girl—Tiffany, maybe—is to my left. The music pounds, and I perform my routine without thought. I unlace the corset, pulling the string hard. I breathe in deeply, grab the pole, kick my leg up and rest my ankle on the cold metal. I'm doing a standing split until I kick up my second leg, wrap it around the pole and hang upside down. The girls are no longer contained by the corset. The guys in front of me stare, lean forward, and toss money my way. I slide down the pole until I'm on the floor, pressing my stomach to the stage. I arch my back and tip my head back. I'm right in front of an older guy. He shoves a twenty in my corset and makes a comment I tune out. I smile coyly at him.

When I'm working, my mind is a million miles away. I'm not teasing some guy I don't know or popping my boobs on purpose. I'm simply not there. So when I sit up and perch on one leg with my hands in front of me like an animal, I no longer feel humiliation.

I feel nothing.

A familiar burn shoots up the leg I'm perched on and I right myself again. I slide my other ankle out, parting my legs in front of a younger guy with a shaved head and a gangly body. There's a piercing on his left lobe and a tattoo wrapping around the back of his neck.

He's watching me without blinking, his mouth watering, thinking about things he'd do to me if we were alone. He holds out a fifty and waves it at me. "Take it off honey and this is yours."

Guys say all sorts of things to me. This one is tame in comparison, but the waving cash never sits right with me. It slams me back into the present and reminds me of what I'm doing. I reach up to the first clasp on the corset and pop it. I work my way down, one by one, unhooking them all. I'm topless, tossing the garment toward the back of the stage. I crawl forward and part my lips, allowing him to put the money between my teeth. I purr when he does it, which makes the guy next to him fish out another twenty. More money juts up from greedy hands surrounding the stage. They all want my attention. They want to make me purr.

They think I'm a goddess, a sex kitten. I never say anything to any of them. I just smile, wink, and lick my lips. My voice would give me away. The shame I feel would be obvious. I'm not some exhibitionist that enjoys swinging on a pole.

I don't know what I am anymore.

I rise and strut slowly back to the pole, money still between my teeth. I'm wearing a black thong, matching thigh highs, garters, and a pair of stilettos. I know which assets guys like the best and work them. Throwing my hip out, I slowly bend to pick up some cash, pushing the curve of my spine out, and making my ass look curvier.

As I pick up the bills and stuff them onto my garter, more money waves in my direction. Coy smile in place, I glance up and freeze.

"I always knew you were a slut, Cassie." Mark is standing there in a cowboy hat, a pair of tight jeans, and a denim jacket with a smug look on his face. "You know what I had to go through to find you. Get your ass down here now. We're leaving. You're my whore, and I don't fucking share." He snaps at me and points to the spot beside him.

I glance around for Bruce. He's not there. The man who's always on the floor, right by the door, isn't there.

Mark knows who I'm looking for. He jabs his thumb towards the door. "That guy is long gone, and if you don't want to find out where he is, I suggest you get your skinny ass down here. Right. Now."

Panic is choking me. The guys around my section of the stage turn toward Mark. The man with the shaved head turns and tells him, "Fuck off!"

Without a word, Mark walks over and cold clocks him. The guy falls on the floor and Mark kicks him in the gut twice. No one says anything. No one helps the man. I stand there, mute, my mouth gaping open.

Mark's beyond pissed now. The veins on his neck are popping up one by one. "Don't make me come up there to get you."

My stomach swirls with ice as I walk to the edge of the stage. Beth calls out to me, "Cassie, don't! Bruce! Where the hell is Bruce!"

People are yelling all around me, but the words sound like buzzing. My heart thumps in my ears, and I break out into a cold sweat. When I get close enough to the edge of the stage, Mark grabs my wrist and jerks me hard. I topple forward, and he lets go. I fall about three feet, landing on my hands and knees next to the guy on the floor. My hair drapes across my face, hiding the thoughts in my head.

Get up before he kicks you.

Run away before he locks you up again.

Fight back before he has his hands on you.

It doesn't matter how much I want to fight. I'm paralyzed. I see the bright lights and hear the blaring horns. Fuck, I even feel the rumble of the massive engine barreling down straight toward me, but there's nothing I can do. It's too late.

Mark's fingers wrap around my arm, and he jerks me to my feet, hissing at me. "You always played the part of the virgin so well, I bought it at first, but you're nothing but a first class skank. I've missed playing our little games, Cassie." His voice drops to a cold whisper. "I brought your favorite."

I can't breathe. A shiver races through me, panic jamming my thoughts. I can feel the metal spikes scraping my skin even though that nightmare happened years ago.

A haze of fear overwhelms me as he shoves me toward the door, not bothering to cover me as he marches me out into the parking lot. I hear Beth screaming, but no one stops him. Why would they? Mark says the same lines he always does—that I'm his wife, a whore who can't get enough. He jokes about locking me up better next time, explains this is a little game we play. They believe him. They always do—why would an honest woman work as a stripper? Why would someone who isn't a sexual deviant be in a place like this?

Tears roll down my cheeks as I stagger, topless, into the parking lot. I'm not moving fast enough, so he grabs my arm to drag me toward his truck. "You stupid bitch. Do you know how much trouble you've caused me?" His hand flies and a sharp slapping sound echoes through the dark parking lot.

My skin stings, but I can't feel it after a second. It's dark, and we're alone. If I fight to get away, I can't run. I'm half naked in heels. Even if I find a cop, he's more likely to arrest me than save me. It's happened before. It only delays the inevitable. Mark bails me out, then does what he wants.

As Mark reaches for the door of the truck, something comes from behind and slams him into the fender. There's a loud crash and a shriek. Beth is there in panties and a bra, holding a pointy heel in her hand like a weapon. "You're not taking her." Breathing hard, she raises the hooker heel to swing at Mark's head.

She caught him by surprise when she body-slammed him into the side of the truck, but Mark sees the shoe coming. He grabs Beth's wrist and twists it so hard there's a crack. She screeches and tries to pull her arm back. I swing at his face, finally coming to life, but he grabs my fist and twists my arm behind my back. I get slammed face first into the side of the truck. He holds me there as he dangles Beth by her broken wrist with his other hand.

He laughs at her. "You pathetic little bitch. You can't hurt me. You couldn't save her even if you pulled a gun out of your ass, you filthy—"

The sound of a weapon cocking cuts Mark's words off cold, but his hands continue to push me firmly against the truck. It's quiet for a moment. "Release both girls and step away." Jon's voice is gravel, tar, and death. I've never heard him like that.

Mark laughs and raises his hands, pulling both of us. Beth screams and tries to kick Mark, but he shoves her down. Beth falls backward and scrapes her elbows on the ground. He acts like it was nothing, like what he did will have no repercussions. It never has before. He drops me, letting me fall to the ground, clapping his hands in Jon's direction as if applauding a theatrical performance. "I have to hand it to you— with ample titties and ass inside and the Ferro name plastered outside, the club certainly isn't hurting for customers. You're a brilliant businessman, Ferro."

Jon aims the gun at Mark's chest. "Shut the fuck up. Cassie, get her inside. Now." I help Beth up and start for the door, but I can't walk away from Jon like this. He never falters, his eyes stay riveted to Mark, but his voice softens. "Please, Cass, just do it."

I help Beth to the door and pull it open. As we cross the threshold, the gun explodes, shattering the night behind us.

CHAPTER 14
JON

Trystan comes around from the back door like I told him. Bob, Trystan's bodyguard, is nearby. That guy is never far away. If he gets here before this asswipe takes off, no one will ever find the body. I consider it. I want Mark to pay for what he did to Cassie. She was frozen with fear when I walked out. Her face was so white she looked like a corpse. I'm not letting him near her again.

Trystan rushes toward me. "Holy shit, you shot him?" We're both staring at the dark stream of blood coming from the guy's leg just above the knee. It soaks his jeans making a big brownish red oval on the denim.

"Walk away, Trystan. There's no reason for both of us to get messed up with this. Odds are someone reported the gunshot. Cops will be here shortly. Move." Trystan rushes off, circling the building to wait out of sight by the side street.

"You just made a mistake, son." That dipshit Mark speaks with a Southern drawl, that good ol' boy thing going on all over the place. I want to beat the crap out of him for that alone. He's a classic prick, the kind of asshole that thinks women are trash. I heard what he said to Cassie and Beth. I knew guys like that. They beat their bitches, using them for pussy then tossing them aside when they finish. I can't comprehend how a girl like Cassie, with her whole virginity-is-sacred thing, ended up with this tool.

I cock the gun again, knowing I'm out of time. "Where's my bouncer?"

"How the fuck should I know?" He's pissed, but still staggering backward, away from me trying to stay clear of the gun.

I lift the weapon. "I don't have time for this, shitface. Where is he?"

He swears and doesn't answer at first. When I rush him and shove the barrel under his jaw, aiming straight up into his skull, he sings a different song. "Behind the trash. He's not dead."

It would be so easy to slide my finger back and pull that trigger. This guy would be out of Cassie's life forever, and she could breathe easy. Forever is a long time. I'd do it for her. I'd end him and not feel a fucking ounce of regret. The guy is a worthless asshole. I'm suddenly aware of how hard I'm pushing the barrel into his skin, and it takes a few breaths, but I manage to pull it away.

I shove him into his truck, hard. "Get the hell out of here, and if I ever see your cock-sucking face again, I'll put a bullet in your fucking skull."

As I lower the gun, pointing it at the ground, that douchebag has the audacity to laugh. "I hear it in your voice, Ferro. You think you can handle her, but you can't. That bitch will stab you in the back if she hasn't already."

I lift the pistol again and aim for his head. "I didn't miss. Your leg was a pity shot, so leave before I change my mind."

*****

The rest of the night races by in a blur. Bob finds Bruce, who, unlike me, has a legal gun. They make up a story and feed it to the cops. Since Bruce has a hole in the side of his head, courtesy of a two by four with a few nails sticking out of the end, the cops don't have issues believing there was a fight. They want to see the other man, though. We tell them he ran after he attacked Beth and broke her wrist. Cassie hides in the dressing room among the other strippers. The police ignore her.

I can see her face. I know those walls shot up so high that they scrape the sky. She's never going to talk to me again. I can't believe that twat got around Bruce. I close the club early, send that blonde to help Beth get her wrist set, and tell everyone else to go home. Trystan hangs around with Bob in case the jackass comes back. Cassie is still here, waiting for me to take her home. I don't want to face her yet. I failed. I let that asshole get to her. He nearly succeeded.

I rub my palms over my face. I'm sitting in the circle of black club chairs next to the stage. The bar is behind me. Trystan walks over with a bottle of bourbon and two glasses. He pours amber liquid into both and hands me one. "Shitty night."

I slam the drink back in one swallow and put the glass down on the table beside me. I glance up at him. "You ever make a promise you can't keep?"

He nods once. "Yep. I have."

I've never heard that story, but he's not offering, so I don't press. "I told her I could keep her safe, but that asshole managed to yank her right off my stage. She shouldn't even be here."

Trystan is sitting across from me, slouched back into the chair, swirling the bourbon around the edge of his glass. "Where should she be?"

"With me, somewhere else. I didn't want this." I point at the walls and stage. "It's a fucking nightmare. There's pussy everywhere, but I don't want any. And her! I sleep next to her, but I can't touch her either. This isn't me. I'm an asshole. I'm selfish. I like to dick around, and somehow I linked myself to a prude stripper with a sociopath husband."

Trystan smirks, his eyes riveted to the whirlpool of liquor. His dark lashes obscure his eyes when he speaks. "That's not why you're mad."

"What?" I snap at him. "I'm a fucking god, and I'm slumming it here with her."

He shakes his head. "This is what love is at its core. You'd do anything for her, even if she doesn't care. Even if she's someone you can never have. For once in your life, your motivation has nothing to do with fucking, and you don't know what to do with it."

I glare at him. "And you do?"

"Not a damned clue. There was this girl a long time ago, but I screwed it up. She's better off without me, but she's always there, in the back of my mind." He looks up at me. "Never before and never since. It doesn't matter how many women I'm with—it doesn't go away."

I pinch the bridge of my nose and swallow hard. "I did this to her. I sent her away without listening. I thought she stabbed me in the back and sold me out."

"She did."

"Did she? The shit the papers printed couldn't have all come from her. I didn't realize it until we spoke again. By then years had passed. Cassie wouldn't have ended up with that guy if I hadn't thrown her out, if I'd just given her a chance to explain."

Trystan leans forward and sets the glass down. "You can't live like that. The wasteland of regret pulls you in and never lets you leave. If you want her, tell her."

I stare at my hands and shake my head. "I can't. He hurt her. She'll never want me like that, and I won't force the issue." I lean back and laugh bitterly. "I'm in love with a woman I can't be with—I can't show her how much I love her. I can't even touch her."

"Do you need to? I mean, think about it. There are other things, right?" I glance at him out the corner of my eye, not following. "There's more to life than fucking, Jon. Meet her where she's at and figure out if that's enough."

The suggestion swims in the grief that fills my mind. Would it be enough? I could just hold her, kiss her, and take what she has to offer when she has it to give. I know that should be enough, but I'm not sure what that looks like. Then my thoughts stumble when I realize that there's one thing I need from her. The rest can fade away, I can live without it, but this—I can't be with her and not touch her. I have to be able to wrap my arms around her and hold her.

Trystan chortles quietly. I glance up at him. "What's so funny?"

"Only that the self-professing male slut found something more important than sex."

CHAPTER 15
CASSIE

I wait in the dressing room until everyone else is long gone. I wipe the makeup off my face and reapply with a lighter hand. I want the ugly red mark on my cheek gone. I want him gone.

I hate what I've become. I can't find my spine when that man is around. I cower, imagining what he'll do to me. The cat claws were the worst. Most women with scars like mine get them during childbirth. I did not. I managed to heal. He did it twice more after that. Blood, sex, and semen are three things Mark likes to do to me.

He was my first. I thought it would be slow and loving, passion and pleasure mixing within us. I had high hopes, none of which turned out to be true. From day one, he hurt. I don't know why, it just did. He got increasingly impatient until sex turned to rape. I was too stupid to know what to do, too scared to ask for help. He was a good man having a bad day. I'd convince myself that it wouldn't happen again.

But it did.

He latched onto the pain and perverted it. He'd tie me down and then jam things inside me—sex toys, bottles, glass—until I passed out. I'd wake up covered in cum and dried blood. Sometimes, toward the end, he'd leave me tied in the basement with no water, nothing to eat for days. I'd scream, but no one ever heard me. When we first moved into that house, he told all the neighbors how amorous I was. 'Insatiable,' he'd say. I thought it was a strange pride at the time, but it wasn't. It gave the neighbors a reason to look the other way when he locked me outside with no clothes, leaving me to freeze on the back porch.

'Sex games,' he'd tell them, 'of course we enjoyed playing and teasing each other.' The way the men looked at me made me afraid to go outside. They thought I'd do anything with anyone. It was so far from where I started, and I felt so incredibly forsaken that I ran away.

The first time I did it wrong. I took things with me and didn't go far enough. He found me, beat me, dragged me home, and we resumed the daily terror that put a grin on his face. He had an iron mask fitted to my head and left me wearing it while he was at work. He used everything from hot wax, to metal claws, to electrified barbs on me. It was a dungeon made for fucking, and he wouldn't let me out.

It never felt good. I never wanted any of it. The thought of going back there terrifies me day and night.

I'm lost in the possible horrors awaiting me and don't see Jon standing in the doorway. His hip rests against the frame, arms folded across his muscular chest. Those blue eyes are dark as the night sky and filled with worry.

He clears his throat and steps into the room. "Are you ready?"

I nod and don't trust myself to talk. What would I say to him? I can't tell him all that. I don't want to relive it. I want it to go away.

He sighs deeply and presses his lips together before finding a seat down the bench. He probably hates me right now. Tonight could have gone a lot worse, and I'm sure he knows it. He rubs his hands on his jeans and glances at me from the corner of his eyes. "I'm sorry."

I can't hide my shock. "For what?"

"For not keeping you safe. For letting that asshole inside. For not stopping him fast enough. For not realizing the extent of what he did to you." His eyes are wide, earnest. He blinks, looks away, and runs his hand over his head and down his neck. "I almost lost you tonight, Cassie, and I was too pissed off about stupid shit."

I look away. I shouldn't have gone nuts on him. He's been so sweet to me, so patient. "It's not stupid to want to do her." I sneer without meaning to when I think about Gretchen.

"Cassie—"

"No, I mean it. I'm sure you're lonely. I would have flipped out less if it had been someone else. Gretchen isn't my favorite person."

Jon loved me that way once, but now he's distant. I feel more like a sister than anything else. It makes me sick inside because I don't feel that way about him. Even conflicted and batshit crazy, I know I want to be with him. I just don't know how. One second it seems like I can handle it and the next it's all I can do to escape.

Jon's voice is deep, soft. "I didn't want to, but I need certain things, Cass, things I can't ask you for."

Oh, God. It feels like he's going to rip my heart out. I can't take it tonight. I can't hear him say those words. I need to make him stall, but there's only one thing that comes to mind. Can I do it? Will he let me? "I understand. You don't have to ask, Jon."

His face scrunches together in confusion. "I don't?"

"No." I'm off the bench and pad to the spot where he sits. I place my hands on his knees and sit between them, facing him. My hands are shaking slightly thinking about it, feeling torn. Before I can change my mind, I reach for the waist of his jeans and undo the button.

"Cass? What are you doing?" He watches me but doesn't stop me.

I don't answer. Instead, I put my fingers on the zipper and pull. His snug black boxers hold his package close to his body. I trace the tip of my finger over the bulge on top of the fabric. Jon closes his eyes, tips back his head, and moans. His breathing seems louder, less controlled. I reach for the elastic band on his shorts to free him, while considering putting him in my mouth. I can do it. I have before. I don't like it, but he needs it. I'm willing to do it for him, regardless.

That's when he grabs my hand and stops me. "Cassie, don't." His voice is so soft, so incredibly careful.

I try to pull my hands back, but he holds on. "I thought you'd like it."

"I don't know what to say." The way he looks at me destroys me. It's like he has no interest in me that way, no matter what the bulge in his pants proclaims.

"Don't say anything. Let me do it." I chance looking up at him and instantly wish I hadn't.

He lifts both my hands to his lips and kisses my fingertips. "I can't. Not tonight." He drops my hands, stands, and kisses the top of my head. As he walks away, he zips up. "Come on. I'll take you home."

CHAPTER 16
JON

I keep dreaming about that night, with Cassie on her knees at my feet, her small body between my legs and that sinful mouth offering to suck me off. I groan and roll over. I've been sleeping on her floor for the past few weeks. Cassie comes to work smiling, does her job—which I can't stand—then goes home with Beth. I follow shortly after.

STRIPPED 2

I can't get her to move to my apartment or quit. I don't want to pressure her because of her relationship with the asshole, but I'm going to lose it soon. I need her. I need to feel her naked body pressed against mine. I want to feel the heat from her inner thighs as she straddles my face and I slide my tongue deep inside her. I want to drink her in, and hold her hips down as she rocks against my face.

I need her. I don't know how else to say it. It's not about fucking or getting off. This is about me and Cassie and our two bodies tangled together into one.

I rub my eyes with the back of my hand and pad out of the tiny room. Beth sleeps in the other closet of a bedroom, leaving the combined living room and kitchen area open at night. There's no TV, just an old couch that smells like cats and mildew. There's a print on the wall, stuck there with tape. It's a riverbank in Paris, the yellow lights glowing softly along the Seine. I've been there. This image is a romanticized version of it, the trees dripping with rich autumn golds.

"That painting makes her so happy. You'd think she won the lotto the day she brought it home." Beth is there, standing behind me in thick oversized socks that go halfway up her calves and a long t-shirt that drowns her. It must have been white at one point, but now it's dingy gray like her socks. The cast on her wrist is covered in glittering pink Duct Tape. She would never have bought it—Beth doesn't spend a dime unless it's absolutely vital—so I bought her four rolls. I think she's taped everything. Her door is pink, her chair is pink, and the old coffee table they found on the side of the highway is also covered with pink tape. I've never seen someone so grateful for something in my life.

My last name affords me everything I want, whenever I want it. I've never had to save and always have more than I could use. Fuck, I have more than I could spend in my lifetime. The concept of being excited about tape eludes me. I wish I could find that much happiness in something so simple.

"She never talks about it." I tip my head toward the painting and follow her to the cockeyed kitchenette table.

Beth grabs the milk and two cups, pouring one for me without asking. "To you."

"Why not?"

"She figures you've been there and doesn't want to sound like a peasant." She grins and hands me the glass.

"Do I sound like that?"

"I don't think so," she says, shaking her head. "You've been sleeping on the floor for weeks without trying to get in that girl's pants. You know what that means." She puts the glass to her lips and chugs the rest of the white liquid.

"No clue."

Slamming the glass on the table, she smiles and sighs like milk is liquid sex. "You're either gay, hard up—since you're a

Ferro, I ruled that option out—or the L-bomb is floating around in your head."

"I already told her I love her. She wasn't interested."

Beth's face scrunches making her mousy features pointier. "You said what?"

I tap my fingers on the side of the glass, feeling the cold condensation under my fingertips. "I professed my undying love, and she said she loved me, too."

"And you're sleeping on the floor?"

"Correct."

She studies me for a moment, the corner of her mouth pulling up into a crooked grin. "God! You mean it, don't you?"

I don't reply.

"She's been through a lot of shit. She doesn't talk about it, but I know she's not dead inside." Beth pulls her feet up onto the chair and wraps her arms around her ankles. She watches me, her dark eyes studying my face, then dropping to my hands on the glass. "So, you're just going to sleep on the floor forever?"

"I don't know."

"Have you talked to her?"

"No, and I'm not going to either."

"Why not?"

"Because of the way we met, okay. I was all about fucking, and she wasn't interested. I charmed her every day and tried to get into her pants every night. It was a game. I don't want her to think I'm playing around. I'm not. I'm worried I lost her, that Mark showed up and, although Cassie stayed with me, he stole what remained of her." I glance up at Beth. "If you tell her any of this, I'll deny it."

She frowns and exhales slowly. Her gaze cuts to the side and then at my glass of milk. "Fine, I won't say anything. Are you going to drink that?" I push the glass toward her. Beth lifts it and guzzles.

"I've never seen someone like milk that much who wasn't, you know, five."

She leans forward and presses her palms to the table. "Ooh! You know what's even better? Chocolate milk! I'm getting me some of that tomorrow."

"I wish I had your zeal."

"No one matches my passion for dairy products."

The corner of my mouth lifts slightly. "Or tape."

She lifts a finger, pauses, and nods. "Glitter tape. If it were invisible tape, it wouldn't matter so much. You'd have more gusto about something you truly want but have to earn."

"You didn't earn the tape."

She smiles at me softly. "Yeah, but I know what it's worth and that it was something I'd never have. You made that possible, Jonny boy." She ruffles my hair as she walks back to her bedroom. She stops in the doorway and looks back at me. "She's lucky to have you."

"That's the first time anyone said that."

"It won't be the last."

CHAPTER 17
JON

The next morning Beth heads out to run, and I'm alone with Cassie. I spent the night on the couch, screwing around on Reddit. I started out laughing at posts about crazy horse girls, then moved to something that hits a little closer to home—dating someone who has been sexually abused. From what I read, it sounds like I'm handling things right. It also sounds like I'm fighting for something that might not be possible. At some point, people become too wounded. They wither and die. What's left is a shell of the person who used to be there going through the motions of life. They slip into a place where no one can hurt them again, but that place prevents them from feeling anything at all. Numbness swallows them whole, and it sounds like a lonely life.

The guys who love women like that sound like martyrs. They give up all physical contact, sleeping in different beds, even different rooms. They live next to her never touching her. Some of their stories get better. Over time, some couples build healthy physical relationships. I find comfort in those endings. But there's something worse. Depression can take over and walk her off a bridge.

It kills me, but I keep reading. It's the same story over and over again. An asshole mistreats a woman for so long she stops fighting. Even if she wants to break free of him, he won't let her go. She accepts her fate. His abuse never ends, until one day she has an opportunity to leave. She takes it, manages to find real love, but she can't forget the abuse, can't believe she didn't deserve it. Suicide pops up over and over again. In the end, the good guy, the guy fighting daily to prove his love earns nothing but gut-wrenching loss.

All his sacrifice is pointless.

Nothing can heal her.

I don't know how far gone Cassie is. I don't know what he did to her, if every aspect of physical contact is ruined, or if it's only sex. I think I could live without it, pretend it isn't important. Dozens of other men said the same thing online. They gave up everything, and a lucky few got the girl back. There are always demons in tow, but everyone has baggage.

My past also lingers in the shadows, tainting my present.

I glance at the picture on the wall. If she bought that, there's got to be some hope floating around inside of her. That picture is Cassie's glitter tape, her milk. She pads out every morning and sits on the couch, staring at it while she drinks her coffee. It's a small thing, but I'll take any flicker of hope that I can get.

I'm not the knight in shining armor. I'm not the hero who saves the girl. I'm the asshole who rips bodices and ravages wanton women. Sometimes I think fate played a cruel trick on me, putting us together. We don't fit and never have. I thrive on sex, and she doesn't want anything to do with it.

Cassie yawns and walks out of the bedroom behind me. She wakes at the same time every day, no matter what. She clings to that schedule of hers like a life raft. In many ways, I guess it is. I feel like a dick for not seeing it sooner, how hard she clings to her life, trying to pull herself back up over the cliff. When you're hanging on by your fingernails, it's not easy.

She's wearing a pajama set I gave her. I was going nuts sleeping near her in those threadbare shirts with nothing between me and her panties. This set is pink stripes with a pink patch on the boob. Her hair is tied into a ponytail on top of her head. She looks perfectly sleepy, still peaceful. Nightmares didn't wake her today.

Previously, she tried to hide them—and I let her. Then Mark stopped by the club and provided a face to the monsters again. It's easier to imagine what she sees while she's dreaming. I finally admitted I have dreams, too. I wasn't lying. I don't have to make shit up around her. I've kept that part of my life hidden from her, and mine was a different experience, but years later the ripples look the same. Nightmares, sweats, aversions to certain things...

I hold a mug of black coffee up over my head so she can take it as she passes. She removes it from my hand, and I drop my arm as she sits next to me on the couch. Her bare knee is close enough to touch, but I don't. She has to come to me—and it can't be with a can-I-give-you-head request. It's like starting over with a twitchy virgin, which is pretty much how she was when I met her. If we start over, it'll be at the beginning.

"Thank you." Her voice is smooth, thick from slumber. She has a serene look on her face as she stares at the picture. It's too small, too far away, but that doesn't seem to bother her. As she sips her coffee, her eyes cut to the side, and she blinks at me. Sheepishly, she lowers the cup and points at the picture. "TV is pretty good this morning."

"Yes, it is. I love this show."

"You would." She giggles. The sound fills me, and I'm greedy for more.

"Why is that?"

She gestures toward the picture. "It's The Sweater Slut in Paris—sexy news at sexy times." She says the last part in a deep, manly voice.

"I didn't realize the sweater slut was a hermaphrodite."

She laughs and nearly spews her drink. She slaps my arm with the back of her hand. "You know you like her."

I'm quiet for a moment, watching the smile fade from her face. I want to ask her, but I can't hear the answer be no. I have no idea what she thinks of me, even after offering me a blowjob. How fucked up is that?

I decide against it. I don't want to know.

"Hey, Cass, come out with me today. Skip work."

"I can't. I need to pay rent."

"You already cleared it. Come on. You haven't had a day off in forever, besides, being your boss has got to have some perks."

She smiles suspiciously. "You don't have to hang out with me, Jon. I know you have other things to do."

"Nope. I really don't. You're the only thing I want to do today." I grin brightly at her and stand, offering her my hand.

"I'm a thing?" She sounds offended.

"The prettiest thing in pink pajamas." She swats at me again. I take her hand, intertwine our fingers and hold her for a second. "Come on. Say yes."

No stripping. No strutting. No naked Cassie with plastic smiles and dead eyes. I want to make her laugh. I want to see the girl I once knew come to the surface again. I'm not an idiot, I know I can't hold her there, but I have to try.

She looks at my hand holding hers and flexes her fingers, tapping the back of my hand one finger at a time. I wish I knew what she was thinking about. Cassie glances up at me with those dark eyes and nods. "I'd like that. Are you sure someone can cover for me?"

"It's already done. There's a line of girls waiting to take your spot." Over the past few weeks, I've turned away more strippers than I could shake a really big stick at—my reputation is spreading. Club Ferro is a safe place to work with no bullshit and good pay. It made me wonder what else I could manage.

She frowns lightly. "Are you going to give my job away?"

I kiss the top of her knuckles. She doesn't flinch, but she doesn't act like she felt it either. "No. I promised it's yours as long as you want it." I watch her, wishing to God she'd say she doesn't want to do it anymore. For no reason I can fathom, she stays. She keeps working, and won't leave. Beth doesn't know why either.

Cassie bobs her head up and down. "You think I'm weird, right? Not wanting sex, but working a job like mine?"

She asked me this once before, then changed the topic, killing the conversation before it started. "Yeah, I think you're weird. I've always thought that. You were the proudest virgin I'd ever met. Life got in the way, but you kicked ass. Now you do what you want."

She watches me from beneath those dark lashes, perched on the couch next to me, clasping the coffee between her hands. "What about you?"

"What about me?"

"Do you know what you want?" her eyes drop to her coffee. "I know you, Jon. You weren't meant to be alone so often. You weren't meant to be the kind of guy who sleeps on the floor. I feel really bad about it, but you won't leave, and I can't throw you out."

"Why not?"

"Beth would kill me. Glitter tape and milk? She'd marry you today if you asked her."

I laugh lightly, smiling. "I've got my eye on someone else."

"Who?" She watches me too long, too intensely. Her lashes flutter, and I think she's watching my mouth between glances at her cup.

Every fucking thing I read said not to tell her. It'll add pressure and that's bad. Be her friend, no strings. No sex. Nothing. She has to come to me.

So I lie. "You don't know her."

"Jon, you're sleeping here. She's going to flip out. I would. Maybe you should spend the day with her instead."

"Cassie."

"I mean it. You're too nice to me. I don't want to screw things up for you. Go on. Go home." She leans closer to push me, but our fingers are tangled.

Her eyes look glassy, and when she gets this close to me, I can't help it. My head sways toward her, inching closer to her mouth. The pull to her is stronger than it ever was before. My gaze remains locked on her lips, wishing I could taste her, to slowly suck on that bottom lip, pulling it into my mouth and nipping it with my teeth.

It turns out I can protect Cassie from everything except me. I exhale loudly and laugh. It's completely inappropriate, and makes her frown. When I start to pull away, she tugs me back, pulling my hand.

Nose to nose, she says, "I shouldn't want you sleeping so close to me, but I do. I shouldn't want to touch you, but I do. You shouldn't be here with me. I don't want to make you lose a girl you obviously care about very much." Her eyes are full of tears. A big one rolls down her cheek, and she smiles, looking away from me.

Fuck it. I can't do this to her either. Navigating all this shit is a nightmare. I'm tired of lingering and waiting. I want to help her, and this feels passive, like it's not doing anything.

I touch the side of her face lightly, turning her back to me. "I do care about her. I love her. I told her, and she said she loved me too, but nothing ever came of it."

Her bottom lip juts out and quivers. "Oh?" Her nose scrunches and her face wrinkles like she's going to start crying.

"Cass, it's you. I love you." I rub my thumbs over her cheeks, pushing the tears away.

"I thought you wanted Gretchen?"

"What? Why would you think that?"

"She said you'd been together, that she did things to you—things that sound like you—so I thought..." She shrugs and watches me carefully with tears building up to replace the old ones.

"I wasn't with her. In any sense. Ever. She tried to get into my pants, but I said no."

She recoils. "You said no?"

"Is that so hard to believe?"

"Yes. What happened to the more sex, the merrier? Where'd that guy go?"

"He grew up, Cass. He regrets not keeping the virgin by his side. He regrets everything."

"So do I."

I lean in closer to wrap my arms around her, and hug her, but Cassie lifts her chin and presses her mouth to mine. The kiss feels so heated, so charged that it's hard to keep calm. I have no clue what just happened, but Cassie is kissing me, and that's all that matters.

She starts laughing and buries her face in my shoulder. "I thought you guys were together."

"Why would I be sleeping here, then?"

She shrugs. "I don't know. Because you're Jon Ferro? No one knows what you're doing."

"I only want you, Cass. I've wanted you from the moment we met and never stopped." She smiles at me so brightly it's contagious. She throws her arms around me and presses her body against mine, hugging me hard. Nothing ever felt so fucking good.

Cassie's my glitter tape, the thing that makes me happy, the thing so far out of reach I thought I'd never have her.

CHAPTER 18
CASSIE

Jon drives into the city and parks in front of a store where half a dozen male forms sport the latest designer looks. I glance at the pizza shop next door and assume we're headed in there. Jon races around to open my door as a valet waits to take the car. Jon holds out his hand and smiles down at me. I slip my palm into his, and he helps me out. The little sports car sits low to the ground and, since I'm wearing a sundress, it's difficult to get out without flashing everyone on the sidewalk.

Seriously, the dichotomy between when to expose myself and when to keep it covered should have me acting like a crazy person by now. Maybe I crossed the line a long time ago, and it's so far behind me I can no longer see it.

Jon's thumb rubs the back of my hand, and he watches me for a moment. His blue eyes are flicking between our hands and my face. He's wearing a sapphire-colored button-down shirt tucked into a pair of slim-fitting black pants. With his other hand, he tugs against the open collar at his neck. He clears his throat before saying, "I need to ask you something. I didn't want to put any pressure on you, and things with my family are shit right now, but I have to—I need to be there for Pete. He's getting married, and I'm a groomsman."

I glance up at the tux shop again, and it dawns on me that he must need to run inside for a fitting or to pick something out. "Right. I nearly forgot. Peter seems like a nice guy. He obviously loves Sidney."

"He does." Jon's eyes are on the side of my face. I drop his hand and take a step toward the window, studying the woven textures, pinstripes, and varying shades of gray. My wedding pops into my mind, unbidden, and I banish the thought before it fully materializes.

Jon steps up next to me. I glance down at the sidewalk and his shiny black shoes. He wanted to get dressed up today. Actually, I didn't realize he planned to look so fancy. Feeling a little self-conscious, I was surprised when he handed me a dress bag and asked if I'd want to wear its contents. When I unzipped it to reveal the dress inside, I nearly cried. His gift is a perfect mix of past and present. Cut from seersucker fabric, the cotton sundress is ruched across the chest and bodice, with tiny rosebuds spilling across the skirt. A wide, feminine ruffle swishes from the hem just above my knee. Miniature daisies are embroidered on the straps and scattered along the neckline. He removed the tags, but I know it's not from G&G, where everything is less than twenty bucks. The bag this dress arrived in probably cost more than that.

It's so pretty and soft that it makes me feel something I haven't experienced in a long time. Now, as I gaze into the store window, enjoying the sensation of the soft fabric caressing my thighs as I move, I feel the rest of it. It's not only the appeal of looking ahead and hoping for the best, but it's also living in the moment without worry. It's as if I stepped out of the shower and stayed clean. There's no residue from my past clinging to me like old grime. The things I've done, the situations I've endured, they leave a haze that doesn't scrub away. It lingers and grows.

Some people can't endure it. They fall and never come up for air again.

I've been bobbing somewhere in the middle for a long time. Today I don't feel like I'm bobbing, no more gasping for air before I sink again. I feel good, and I know why.

It's Jon.

The way he treats me is refreshing. I'm not a skank, but I'm not the nun I used to be. To him, I'm Cassie. No strings, no labels, and no treating me like I might break. At the same time, he doesn't belittle what's happened to me, what I've experienced. It's like he understands on some level. Maybe it's empathy, but I suspect there's more story there—something he's not told me—an incident that happened a long time ago, changing him. There are moments in life that alter everything. I know. I feel like I'm standing in one now.

Jon slips his hands into his pockets, pushing back the cuffs on his shirt to reveal a chunky watch. It's white and rose gold with exposed gears. I don't recognize the brand. It's French, something I'd never see, never mind own. It suits him. I glance up at his clean-shaven face, which is a rare sight to see. His usual grin is gone, and I feel the tension flowing from his body. He wants to say something but seems hesitant.

"What is it?" I turn toward him. "Your mother won't keep you out. Peter won't let that happen." I guess at his concerns but miss the mark. I can tell by the way his lips part and then close again.

He glances at the shop window, then cuts his eyes back toward me. "It's not that."

"Then what is it?"

"I don't have a date. I never asked anyone. Someone from my past appeared, and I couldn't think of anything else. Then more shit happened and the next thing I know, I'm standing with you outside the tux shop a few days before the wedding, wondering how the hell I'm supposed to ask you." The corner of his mouth pulls up on one side as he speaks, and it sounds like he wants to laugh it off but can't. Those bright blue eyes lock on mine. Vulnerability spreads across his beautiful face as he tucks his chin and finally asks, "Cassie, will you be my date?"

It's sweet and incredibly unlike him to be anything but confident. I take his hand, lean in and peck his cheek. He could have said any other word, but he chose 'date.'

"I'd love to go with you. I can discuss the weather with your mother. It'll be awesome." I joke about the sore spot and squeeze his hand.

Relief washes over his face, and he looks down at me. "You make everything awesome, Cass."

A smile spreads across my face, and I wish he'd kiss me, but he doesn't. He stands there, watching me in a way I can't understand. It's equal parts affection and distance. I wonder about kissing him again, but I can't understand why he's not touching me. He said he was interested in me, but he's not acting like it. Old Jon would have been trying to talk me out of my panties from the first second. This man doesn't do that. It's like he's going slow on purpose.

I need to stop over-thinking everything. My emotions have been shocked too many times, too close together. It's like my heart took a flying leap onto the third rail and stayed there. It shorted out my ability to sort through everyday feelings, disconnecting and jumbling everything.

I take his hand again, wanting more of his tender touches. I weave our fingers together and enjoy the sensation of warm skin on skin. It's okay to revel in it, to enjoy it at face value. For once, a person in my life doesn't have an ulterior motive to be here, to want to know me. I can't concoct one that would have him sleeping on the floor this long, dealing with a neurotic girl that runs hot and cold all the time. Nothing is worth the trouble I put him through, the pain I cause, and yet—

when he looks at me like that from beneath those dark, thick lashes, I melt.

Does it matter why he's here? Can't I just enjoy the moment? That's all life is, a series of moments scattering to the wind on a whim. At times, getting from dawn to dusk is hard enough. I can't think ahead at all. I'm always running, even in my mind, racing through life trying not to feel anything anymore. I can't take another heartache. I can't fathom surviving another devastating loss. I should push him away, make him keep his distance.

It's safer. It's smarter.

But it doesn't lead anywhere. This path dead-ends with me alone, forced into a cul-de-sac of regret.

"Cass?" Jon's voice pulls me from my thoughts.

"Yeah?"

"You're thinking too much."

"No, I'm not." I smirk at him and duck my eyes to the side. "I'm just pondering."

"All right. I'll bite. What are you pondering, Miss Hale?"

I make a face. "You sound like Sean when you speak like that."

"God knows we don't want that!" He chuckles, tucking his arms into the crooks of his elbows and leaning his shoulder against the brick on the storefront next to the window. "Spill. Inquiring minds want to know."

My fingers play with the flowing fabric of my skirt. I look down at the pavement, watching the ruffles wiggle as I swish the fabric while I speak. "Have you ever wondered what your life would be like— who you would have been—if a certain crappy event hadn't happened?"

I glance up at him in time to watch his face fall. He nods once.

"I do that a lot, and if I'm not careful, I get stuck there, wondering about things that will never happen. My life went down a different road I would have never taken.

I mean, who wants to roll around naked in a cactus field for years?"

Jon smiles, tucks his chin, and lifts his eyes to mine. His guard is up, but he seems like he's trying to fight it back down. Like he's not sure where I'm going with this.

"It hurts. I'm covered in scars no one can see, but for once—without even trying—I feel normal. Standing in front of a shop in this dress, talking about your brother's wedding," I shrug my shoulders and let out a content sigh. "It's something from the normal road. No cactus patches in sight. I'm not sure how I got here, but I'm glad I am, and I'm happy that it's with you."

CHAPTER 19
JON

That confession makes me want to rip my hands out of my pockets and throw my arms around her. I'd never let go, so I make fists and leave them there. Before I met Cassie, I thought I had no self-restraint. The truth is I never needed it. I took what I wanted, no waiting required. But it's never been that way with Cassie. The game faded fast, and I'd do anything for her because I want to. The conquest lost its thrill when I started to care about her. The entire situation changed.

I changed.

Now I need to make my family accept it. They still see the old version of me, and I suspect they will for some time, but Cassie is part of my life. She's not leaving and if they chase her off things won't end well. I know myself, now. I know where I stand. Before this, I wasn't willing to fight for much, but Cassie shifted my outlook on the world, and I won't back down.

There's always been a discrepancy that bothered me in Cassie's story about the reporter. I figured she just didn't want to admit to telling them everything, but now I'm not sure. In the past I accepted my family at face value, but not anymore. Sean is pissed at me and will do anything to get what he wants. He's a clone of my mother and, from what I can tell, the two of them are working against each other, gearing up for World War III.

I never saw my father as a threat, but I'm no longer confident in that assumption either. The story in the paper included the mistresses, both that he had them and that mom allowed it, but the story skipped the part about me screwing my father's women. I thought it would be there, but that part was missing. I always thought Cassie was holding that card, waiting to play it if she ever needed to. But it never happened.

I swallow hard and look at her. I'm way off my normal path, too, and for once I'm not staring at the scenery. I'm intently focused on what lies ahead and the woman standing in front of me.

"I love you, Cass. You have no idea how much." I try not to smile at her with a full-on toothy grin because I'll look like a fucking lunatic, but I want to. My entire body is vibrating with a glee I can't act on.

She returns a shy giddy gaze. "I love you, too." Her cheeks redden and she drops her lashes, hiding her eyes, and grinning at the street.

My chest is ready to burst. I'm normally an emotional vacuum—at least, I try to be—but Cassie has me strung high, and I don't want to come down. Ever. I press my lips together and hold out my hand. "Pick out a tux with me, and then I have a surprise for you."

She lifts a brow at me while placing her hand in mine. "Really?"

"Yeah, but you're going to have to hang around with me all day and part of the evening."

She pushes out that plump bottom lip. "Tonight too? But I wanted to see my other boyfriend after this."

I can't help it. I rip my hands out of my pockets and grab her, pulling her close. I blast her with my most charming smile. "Your other boyfriend doesn't stand a chance against me."

"Oh?"

"Oh. This surprise is that good. You're going to love it."

"That's a lot of talk, Ferro. Are you sure it'll live up to the hype?"

I press my head to hers and feel her little nose against mine. "All that and more."

*****

The tux shop has my new Kiton ready, and Cassie nearly chokes when she hears the price. Her eyes are dinner-plate-sized, and she leans toward me, whispering, "How are you able to buy this?"

It's a fifty thousand dollar custom-made tux. We're at the flagship store on 54th Street in Manhattan for the final fitting before I can take the thing home. We've been standing near a small display of about ten jackets, each perfectly pressed and perched on thick wood hangers. The tags have no prices, and she finally asks about it.

I tell her, "When you're in a place like this, money isn't an issue. You're here because you want the prestige that comes with the brand."

I sound like an asshole, but money takes on a different feel when you have more than you could spend. Five grand feels like five bucks, so a fifty thousand dollar suit doesn't make me blink.

Cassie looks like she's ready to hurl. "Jon, they cut you off. I don't understand. Did you buy this before that happened?"

"Not exactly. It was ordered, not paid for." She turns greener. I smile over at her. "I'm glad you're concerned about my welfare, but I'm not destitute. Besides, it's for Pete's wedding. I can't show up wearing something off the rack and get shown up by the turkey vulture's tuxedo." Crazy though it sounds, Sydney plans for that bird to waddle down the aisle with her. A smile creeps across my face as I imagine my mother's reaction.

"You're not?" Cassie's voice snaps me back to the present. "I thought you were broke."

I didn't say anything about it because she works so hard and I didn't want to come off sounding like an asshole. It's difficult to fight preconceived notions, plus I've been a total dick so often that those perceptions aren't unfounded.

I hold out my hand for her and she slips her palm into mine. We wander over to a set of leather club chairs in the center of the room. I think they were made in Naples along with the rest of the stuff in here. They're a shade of green that matches Cassie's worried pallor, and surrounded by dark wood walls. It's a dude store. It smells manly. The chairs are supple and comfortable. The thick rug beneath my feet is hand woven and cost a fortune. I know because a similar one graced the floor of my room at the mansion. I haven't been back there since the night I bought the club. Mom may have torched it in my absence.

Claiming to have no money in a place like this will spread rumors faster than anything. I lower my voice when I speak. "Cass, I'm fine. I had assets in my name. I lost the inheritance, but that's it. I have other forms of income."

She blinks at me. "You do?"

I laugh. "Yeah, what do you think I do all day?"

"Hang out at a strip club."

I watch her, wondering what she really thinks of me. Gazing into those brown eyes, I can see her affection, but the money is an issue. She missed something, and I kind of hid it from her. I wonder if she's going to be pissed. I might as well tell her. "The club is a novelty endeavor I took on the side. I have a few other businesses going, most of which began to thrive after I met you. There's the private school in Jersey I already told you about. We've been using that as the flagship school, trying new ways of teaching, and experimenting with curriculums. Affluent families like that. There are three established so far, two more coming. That's a large source of my income. I have some traditional financial investments— stocks, bonds and mutual funds I picked up over the years—along with some other ventures that maintain a decent return. I own a hotel on Madison Avenue, a string of vacation homes in the Hamptons, and some commercial property on Long Island I can sell off if I ever need to. I don't need to, so I've been leasing it out for different events..." I trail off when I notice she's gaping at me. "What'd I say to make you stare at me like that?"

Her jaw flops around like a fish, and she sputters, "You've been sleeping on my floor. You've been wearing cheap clothes. You made a big deal about buying Beth tape. I thought you were poor!"

The corners of my mouth lift. "I made a big deal about the tape because she wanted it so much. Plus, it was fourteen dollars a roll, and there was nothing on it. The silver duct tape is less than half that price with twice as much tape."

Her jaw is still dangling open. I reach out, press my finger to her chin, and press it shut. She swats my hands away. "You have money?"

I nod. "Yeah."

"You're not poor?"

"Far from it."

"And you've been sleeping on my floor?"

"Yes." I'm not sure what's happening. She's pissed or ready to cry. I can't tell which one.

She starts to talk and stops, gets up, walks in a circle, and then comes back. Palms out she tries again and stumbles over her words. "I thought. You said. The club, and," she tugs her hair and then leans over, places both hands on the arms of my chair and stops an inch from my face. "You sleep on the floor?"

It sounds like a question, and I admit I'm a little terrified. She's an emotional whirlwind. I'm concerned about what's going to come out when she can finally speak. "I do. You knew I was there, didn't you?" I tease playfully, hoping for a smile.

Her bottom lip curves up in the center, down at the corners and her eyes fill with tears. Shit.

Her voice shakes when she spills her thoughts on me. "I thought you were broke. I thought you were sleeping at my place because you'd been disowned and had nowhere else to go. I thought you stayed on the floor and didn't buy a mattress because you had no money. You stayed there so long." Tears roll down her pale skin and drip off her cheeks as she realizes what I was doing—why I slept there night after night.

Her glassy eyes meet mine and hold. Her lips part as she blinks back tears. I don't know what to do. I thought she knew, but it appears that she had no clue at all.

Cassie thought I was penniless and needed a place to stay. She opened her door to me and shared what little she had. It's clear she never saw this coming, but I don't know how. I slept next to her, on her floor. There was a cat-scented couch a few feet away that would have been a lot more comfortable. I was there for her, and now she knows.

Cassie's lips tug at the corners, twitch, and fall. It's like she doesn't know if she should laugh, cry, or scream at me. She's nodding and pointing a finger at me when she speaks. "You stayed there for me? You slept like that for me? You could have left. You could have bought anything you wanted, but you didn't."

"I wanted to be there."

She echoes me, shocked. "You wanted to be there?"

I pull her onto my lap and hold her against me. Cassie tips her head to the side and rests it against my shoulder. "I'd do anything for you, Cass. I thought it was what you needed. You wouldn't talk to me about work, and I couldn't make you stop."

She straightens and looks down at me. "I thought we needed the money."

I move my head a bit and catch her eye. "You insisted on working because of me? Cass, I own the club. Why'd you think I was broke? At the very least there was income from that."

She waves me off. "That place was barely floating before you showed up. Then, you started giving paid days off and sick time. I thought you were hemorrhaging cash. You're too nice to be a boss. I thought you'd lost your business sense when you purchased the club."

I laugh. I don't mean to, but I can't help it. I kiss her forehead and squeeze her tight. "You pegged me perfectly with everything except the business aspect. I've always been about the sale, Cass. You should know that better than anyone. Once I figured out how to tie income to that ability, it was a like a golden carrot dangling in my face. I had to have it."

"So, you're still rich?"

"Yeah."

"Like moderately wealthy?"

"Cassie, millionaires don't shop here."

"You're a billionaire? Really?" She's shocked, staring at me with her jaw dangling open.

"Yes. What's the matter? Is that bad?"

She starts crying again and swats at her eyes. "A billionaire sleeps on my floor."

"I love you, Cassie. I'd sleep on a bed of nails to be near you."

She smiles at me through the tears, and I want to stay like this forever. In that moment, she sees me, all of me, and I fucking love it.

CHAPTER 20
JON

We drive down a few blocks to a Midtown heliport. Cassie blinks at me as I coax her inside.

"But where's the pilot?"

"You're looking at him." I grab my headset and start pre-flight checks.

I feel her eyes on the side of my face. She says something, but I can't hear her while wearing the headset. I reach across and flick on her microphone. "Say that again."

"Where's the cocky slacker version of Jon Ferro?"

I laugh. "Back in high school where he belongs. Did you really think I'd put all my eggs in one basket? You saw who holds the handles, right? My parents are insane." I swallow the rest of my reasons before they come rushing out. She's not certain of me anymore. This doesn't mesh with what she knows about me, but that was years ago.

I didn't stop living when we parted ways. If anything, I pulled my shit together because of her. I realized my mother could cut me off at her whim, so I took my money and stopped dicking around. I sold off the toys, invested here and there, and figured out what I needed to do.

The pilot's license was a necessary evil. If I needed to cut my budget, I didn't want to get stuck flying commercial between my businesses, wasting time with airport security and delays. After getting those licenses, it seemed stupid to skip the helicopter certification. It's helpful to be able to dart above the city—especially at rush hour. So, I bought a few planes, a jet, the helicopter, and started another business offering private flights to individuals and companies who don't want to deal with owning an aircraft. Everything I possess is dual purpose, making life easier while making money. I hate to admit it, but I learned that from Dad.

That man is a genius. Everyone thinks Mom came with an endless pile of cash, but Dad's the one that keeps a large portion of it regenerating. I didn't understand until I got back from that summer with Cassie and caught hell from Mom. After, Dad called me into his office— which I'd always thought was there for show—and sat me down. I expected him to finish tearing me a new one, but, instead, he asked me about my net value and possessions. He listened thoughtfully as I spoke, then suggested I downsize my jet and lease it when I wasn't using it. He explained in detail how I could earn money from it by providing an economical flight option to time-conscious businessmen, while I stared at him, shocked.

That's why mom doesn't walk away, why she lets him have his affairs. She needs him. She's good at getting her fingers into everything, exerting pressure, and wielding power. Dad's skills, though more subtle, are just as integral to running an empire—which is exactly what they're doing.

"Is this safe?" She glances around, yelling in the headset as she strangles her seat belt.

I continue preparing for lift off and say something to the tower, before answering her. "Perfectly. Sit back and enjoy the ride. It'll only be a few minutes."

"Where are we going?"

"To the yacht club on the upper east side. I'm taking you sailing."

"Ooh! On a boat?" Cass is excited, and when I glance over at her, she's beaming at me.

She makes me laugh. The way she says it isn't condescending. Some men would flinch at the size reference, but I know she would have called the Queen Mary 2 a boat as well. To her, it means floating, and that's fun. I see it in her eyes.

"Yup, on a boat."

CHAPTER 21
CASSIE

The ride over the city was unreal. I've lived here for years without experiencing it like that. Flying in a helicopter isn't the same as a plane. Instead of a rumbling horizontal ascent, you take off vertically like an elevator, shooting up into the sky and soaring over the skyscrapers. Landing is a similarly abrupt plummet through the air before parallel parking between two other helicopters. I was nervous watching Jon do it, but he didn't act like it was a big deal. His confidence has grown up and internalized. He's sure of himself. He doesn't project it the way he did when we were younger. He just knows what to do and does it.

When we land at the heliport, a limo is waiting. We take the short ride to the yacht club. I glance around, seeing famous people and trying not to stare. I look over at Jon across the room. He's speaking with someone, a man, about the yacht.

Jon stands there smiling warmly, one hand in his pocket and a confident look in his eyes. He nods and says something, then waits for a reply. The arrogant boy who never listened is gone. He's soaking up every word the man says.

Jon thanks him and walks back to me. "Ready?"

I nod, stand, and smooth my skirt. "Yup!" I'm too excited to control my grinning. My face starts to ache. When he asked me to go out this morning, I thought he meant McDonald's. I never expected this.

A few minutes later, we're on the boat, and several men help to prep the vessel. Satisfied that everything is in order, the guys from the yacht club disembark and head back to the marina. I watch as Jon alone maneuvers the ship away from the dock in complete control.

As we pull away, we head up the river and toward the Atlantic. I sit there, happy to feel the sun on my face and the spray of salt on my skin. Before we left, Jon pointed out different areas of the ship I might want to explore. I stand, kick off my shoes, and pad around the deck, ducking my head into different cabins and wandering through a large sitting area adjoining a beautiful dining room. I'm watching a chandelier sparkle and sway in time with the water when Jon walks up behind me.

"Are you hungry?"

"Yes, but don't you need to steer?"

He laughs and shakes his head, making that dark hair fall into his eyes. He pushes it back. "No, the ship has automation for that. Dinner was prepared and brought on board before we left. Should we eat in here and then have dessert on the deck after the sun sets?"

It feels like I'm in a dream. "That sounds incredible." As he places the dishes and silverware on the table, I sit and ask him about his businesses, surprised he speaks so freely. He leases this yacht as well. The club cares for it and helps procure lessees. An agent does the rest.

In the middle of our meal I glance up at him. The sun is setting, painting the room with vibrant oranges and yellows. Jon's hair is a mess from the wind and salty spray. It's got a ruffled thing going on that makes my fingers itch to touch it.

Jon glances up at me and places his fork and knife down. "Can I ask you something?" His tone is serious, deeper than usual with less inflection. It's not a question he wants to ask.

"Anything."

"What did you tell that reporter about Dad's mistresses? It's odd how they honed in on my parents' relationship but skimmed over the other more immoral issues there. It was almost as if they didn't know." He watches me carefully beneath those dark lashes. This is a sore spot for him, a festering wound with the blade still buried deep within.

I've always felt horrible about this. I accepted blame for it, but I don't recall mentioning the mistresses. I must have, in passing maybe, without realizing it. Or maybe the guy already had his story and needed someone to corroborate it. Either way, it doesn't matter. It was my fault the story appeared.

"I don't remember. I didn't think I said anything, but I must have."

"You talked mostly about the school and the bombing?"

"The good things about the school and yes, your selflessness during the bombing. That was a story by itself, but he didn't mention any of it. I wanted everyone to see the real you." I smile sadly and stare at the tablecloth. "I didn't even know the real you. I never knew you were capable of all this—the businesses, the analytical stuff, and then not flaunting it."

The corner of his mouth rises slightly and falls. "Fledgling companies are easy to take down. I hid them on purpose so they'd have a chance."

"You're a lot smarter than most people recognize."

"I've realized that, which is why this bothers me. If you mentioned the mistresses, you would have said it in passing, right?" I nod. "So how'd he know about the details of my parents' relationship?"

"Another source?"

"Right, which means he flew down to Mississippi to find you."

"That doesn't make sense either," I say, shaking my head. "This guy followed me for weeks, trying to convince me to talk about you. From what I could tell at the time, he seemed to be a local. At the very least, he was from the South."

Jon stares off, thinking. His hands are on the table, pressing his fingertips against the fabric. He sighs and runs his hands through his hair. "He had to get the information somewhere."

"If not from me, then from where? What are you thinking?"

"I'm thinking there was a pissing match going on between Luke and Mom, and I got in the way."

I want to say no, that it's not possible, but his uncle, though crazy, would not be unjustified in blasting his sister. "Did you ask him?"

Jon's gaze doesn't lift to meet mine. "No. When it first happened, I thought you leaked part of my family stuff on purpose. I kept waiting for you to drop the rest, but you didn't. Luke knew everything. He must have disclosed the parts most damaging to Mom and left out the rest."

His voice sounds lost. His fingers have turned white from pressing them against the table so hard for so long. There's something he thinks I know, something bad, but I don't have any clue what it is. "Jon, I don't think I talked about the mistresses. It was my fault the entire thing happened—I won't say it's not. It is. I did it, and the story wouldn't have appeared without me, but I'm not sure what you're talking about now. You think I figured out something that I don't know."

Jon's gaze lifts and locks with mine. He takes a small breath and watches me, wondering if he should trust me. He thinks I already know some dark secret, but I can't fathom what it could be.

The silence stretches between us, so I say, "You don't have to tell me anything."

He considers it, sits back in his chair, and folds his arms over his chest. "I want honesty. I want all the crap between us gone. I'm tired of assuming you did this when it's possible you didn't. And if you did do it, I want to know. As for my secrets, if you don't know them already, you should." He swallows hard and holds my gaze with an unnerving intensity.

"Some things are hard to talk about."

"I know." He doesn't bark the words, but he doesn't sound too pleasant either.

"Be patient with me, okay?" I ask. "I think I can tell you, but it's not like ripping off a bandage. It's more like stabbing myself in the heart. Ripping everything open again is not something I want to do."

Jon's gaze drops to the table. He nods once. "You ask first."

I wonder how direct I should be, if I should just come out and say it. Jon folds his arms over his chest and waits, not looking up at me.

"What happened when you went home that summer?" My question seems to surprise him.

"My funds were frozen, and my mother publicly emasculated me. She stripped my privileges so I couldn't go about my daily life. Basically, I was locked in the mansion where Mom could make sure nothing else happened. It was very public within the family, a warning to anyone else who might step out of line." There's still pain in his voice. This went beyond humiliation, they did something to him, more than what he's saying. I'll circle back to it.

Jon asks point blank, "Why aren't you divorced?"

"Oh. That."

"Yes, that."

"It's complicated."

"It isn't. Which begs the question, why are you still married to that guy?"

Thoughts flop around in my head, obscuring the real answer. I push the usual responses away and say it. "I'm afraid of him. I'm afraid he'll do something worse, afraid that's even possible, and thought it was better if he didn't know where I was.

Also, I don't have the money. That's not the main reason, though. It never was."

Jon watches me, his eyes boring into mine, sorting through my pain and doubt. It's all there, laid out to be seen and judged. I want to explain, but I keep my mouth shut.

"Thank you," he says softly. "Your turn."

"Why do you hide who you really are? Why not let people see you're smart, shrewd, and loyal? What's with the act you put on day in and day out?" I never judged him for it, nor would I because I do the same thing. For me, it's a defense mechanism, a way to hold myself together. But for him, I don't understand.

His gaze drops and he inhales deeply, then lets it rush out. Jon looks at the window. The sun has almost disappeared beneath the dark blue waves. "I didn't know who I was until after I met you. You introduced me to myself, to a guy I didn't know existed. I didn't like him at first and fought the transition. By the time I figured it out, most people had already pegged me for a can't-do-shit player. Challenging expectations would have caused problems, too, for several reasons. If I act like an airhead, no one looks at me twice. If they know I have Sean's mind and Peter's drive, they'll look hard. I don't want anyone scrutinizing my life."

Everything makes sense except that last part. I'd assume he wanted privacy, but this is Jon Ferro. He likes to show off and be in the limelight, so what's he hiding?

Jon stares past me, out the window and asks. "How'd you find out about my involvement with the mistresses?"

"What do you mean?" I sit forward and watch as he wrestles with this one.

I watch his Adam's apple bob in the center of his throat, and he asks again, "How did you know?"

"I didn't. I suspect I still don't." He's pensive for a moment, leaning on his elbows, his hands propping up his chin. "There's something else about the mistresses, isn't there? Something you don't talk about, something you hope no one knows. What is it?"

When those eyes lift to meet mine, they're cold and hollow. It's like he's caught on train tracks and can't move. The truth is barreling down on him without mercy. He nods, and swallows hard. He's looking at me but doesn't see me. Darkness shadows his features, obscuring his handsome face with pain and regret.

"The first one, Monica." He can barely say her name. It sticks in his throat, practically choking him. His posture remains closed off, and he folds his arms across his chest with an angry scowl on his lips. "She did things, threatened me if I didn't comply. I was barely a teenager and didn't realize her game until it was too late."

"She seduced you?"

He nods. "I said no, but it didn't matter. She kept coming to me. It was flattering at first, but it wasn't something I would have done without her initiative. The things she wanted me to do to her were fucked up. The first time, I barely remember it. She drugged me, and I wasn't myself. The next morning she was gone. I thought it was over, but then she wanted more. I refused and told her to fuck off. Her response was a picture of us shoved under my bedroom door with a note that said, 'Wouldn't it be horrible if this ended up in your mother's room?' She took it that first night we were together. I couldn't say no after that."

Venom spikes to the surface and I want to hurt her. My fingers flex, and it takes a lot to keep my voice even, calm. "She blackmailed you?"

"Yeah, I guess you could say that."

"So, how'd it stop?"

He glances up at me and looks sick. His eyes dart away and sweat breaks out on his brow. "She kept fucking me every few weeks until she got a ring from Dad. After that, she stopped—until the night my mother refused to divorce Dad. All hell broke loose. My parents went insane, in opposite directions, leaving me alone with Monica.

"She was pissed, and the only one available to take it out on was me. I was about to turn fourteen and had no clue how to handle myself. I wouldn't hit her—even when she came at me with a knife. She told me I was just like him, a fucked up perv, and I'd like what was coming to me. She held a blade to my neck and pressed until there was blood. I felt it running hot down my throat.

"Instead of pushing it in the rest of the way, she tossed it on the floor and gave me a choice—sober or wasted. Either way, she wasn't leaving. I took the coward's way out and swallowed a pill that left me more coherent than I wanted. She recorded the entire thing. The blood, the sex, her fucking me so hard it looked like I didn't care. You can't tell I'm out of it, and I remember everything, lying there unable to move while she mutilated me with the knife."

He sucks in a sharp breath and looks directly at me. "I've waited ten years for that tape to go public. I look like a fucking sadist, screwing my dad's fiancée. She made sure her fucking engagement ring stayed in plain sight and said a bunch of shit about screwing all of us together like she was the only woman any Ferro man wanted.

"If that tape pops up, even though she never touched them—I know because Pete was grief-stricken over his first fiancée's death, and Sean was anywhere but here— it could have serious consequences for my brothers. She implies things happened with Sean and Pete even though they didn't. It doesn't matter. It will look true. I look like someone who can't be trusted, ever. And the entire time she was with me, I never thought she'd do anything like that. I underestimated her. I walked into a bear trap, and didn't fucking notice until the metal teeth snapped off my leg."

He's breathing hard, and his hands are clutching the arms of his chair. Jon doesn't look at me. His voice is deep, angry, "Do you still want to be with me? Do you want to be with a guy who won't defend himself? A dickhead who did some seriously fucked up shit with his father's fiancée? That's hanging over my head and always will. If you stay with me, one day it might show up and take us both down."

I'm so horrified I can't speak. He's burning holes into the table with his eyes, expecting an answer that will gut him. He thinks I'll run, that I'll say no.

I'm trembling and just start talking. The words rush out and won't stop. "I thought it was my fault, the stuff with Mark. I thought I didn't know how to do it—how to have sex well enough to satisfy him. I thought it was me. I did anything he wanted. Anything." The last word is a whisper.

Jon lifts his head, his expression softer, and watches as I retell the nightmare that became my life. "It hurt. Sex with Mark always hurt. He wasn't mean at first, but when I asked him to slow down and give me more time, he wouldn't. Eventually, pain and tears were just part of the routine. It pushed him darker until he didn't care what I wanted or how I felt. He'd go from being completely sweet to chasing me down to use me. I couldn't move or throw him off.

"After a while, I tried to run. That made him worse. He locked me up, and he told everyone the same kind of thing he said at the club—that we liked to play these sadistic games. It made my neighbors ignore my screams. No one thought anything if they didn't see me for weeks. We were those people. They never thought I didn't want him. Sex turned to rape. Rape turned to beatings. There are videos of me, too, pictures of me doing things to him."

I swallow hard and steel myself for the rest. "The last time he took me, he... He cut me with a metal claw—inside. I healed, but there are scars, one is really long and jagged. It hurts when I," my jaw opens and closes, but I can't say it.

It's devastating. The scars Mark left cause me pain I can't overcome.

Jon reaches across the table, gently taking my hand. He rubs his thumb across my knuckles. "Cass?"

I force my head back and have trouble meeting his eyes.

"Is Mark the only man you've been with?"

I nod slowly, unable to speak. I feel sick and want to cry, but there are no more tears. Mark ruined me completely.

Jon lifts my hand and places a kiss in the center of my palm. He waits a moment and says carefully, "Have you seen a doctor?"

"No. I healed, but it hurts even when it's just me or a dream." I smile weakly. "I've wanted to do things with you, but I'm afraid. I won't want to stop, and I can't handle the pain. It's not just that it reminds me of him and what he did. Things don't work right anymore." I try to force a smile, but it falls flat.

"I don't want you to do that. I'm glad you didn't, and I'm grateful you told me." Jon's voice is kind. I half expected him to go crazy and threaten to kill Mark, but he doesn't. He remains calmly focused on me.

I nod and try to meet his gaze, but it's hard. My eyes fall on the table and study the woodgrain. I'm acutely aware of my breathing and feel like I'm ready to bolt. Talking about this is beyond difficult. I'd rather have my guts ripped out and be left on the side of the road half alive. When something reminds me of Mark, I'm not dead, but I'm no longer living. I cower when shadows stretch across the ground. I startle at noises in the night. When I first moved in with Beth, I woke her in the middle of the night screaming so loudly she busted into my room with a baseball bat. I swore I'd seen a man standing over me, that the room was so dark I could only see the whites of his eyes. I told her that night what happened, about my nightmares, and that it never stops.

I know my reactions are irrational, and that normal people think I just spook easily, but if you look beneath the surface it's not hard to see. I no longer have the luxury of acting like anything—I only react. I can't seem to get ahead of it and I'm so tired of cowering. Periodically I find strength and plow forward no matter the cost. Those times are few and far between. Working at the strip club reminds me I'm in control of my body now. For me, it's not about sex. It's about power. I decide what I'm willing to do and when I'm willing to do it. It's a deep-seeded psychological reaction to what I've lived through. I don't poke that area of my mind too much. It's barely stable as it is. Sometimes not knowing why I do something is all that holds me together. There is no glitter tape to patch my wounded soul.

Jon is speaking softly, carefully as if he knows I'd bolt if I weren't stuck on a boat. "Cass, I'm saying this for you, not me, but I think you should speak with someone. I know a doctor—one of my cousin Logan's colleagues—who works with rape victims. I've heard her talk about it."

"Have you met her?"

He nods slowly and takes a deep breath. "Yeah, I have. It's kind of an awkward story."

He has my full attention. "You can tell me. I have no right to judge anyone."

My words seem to sadden him, but he doesn't comment on them. He simply continues, "She came to me once, and told me stuff that I didn't want to hear at the time."

"What do you mean?"

"She could tell from my behavior and my body language that someone messed with me—that I was sexually abused. I refused to call it what it was, I still have trouble with that, but she was kind. She was one of the few people who understood my fucking spree wasn't really about sex. I needed a shrink, Cass." He laughs bitterly and runs his hands through his hair and down his neck.

It literally hurts to hear him talk about this. I wish it never happened to him. I wish I could go back and stop it. There's no way to remove the pain of the past, if anyone knows that truth by now, it's me.

Jon continues, "I needed someone to take my head apart and put it back together correctly. My heart left the conversation when that bitch started screwing me. I kept my head in the sand and didn't want to feel anything. Ever. Sex was physical after that, a necessity like food or water. I fucked. It was a game, something to master."

"I remember you saying that."

"I believed it, and if I wanted to keep on living like that, I could. The truth is I still don't want any woman to have the power to destroy me again." He's staring at me, our eyes lock, and it feels like I've been sucker-punched.

Tears spring up in my eyes. How could he say that? After everything I just told him, he reverts to 'a fuck is a fuck?'

"So, we're friends and always will be? Nothing more? Is that what you're saying?" I blink back tears and force a smile, but it won't stay in place. My lip quivers and I start crying. I can't help it. I'm too raw, too exposed. I never saw this coming.

Jon rushes around the table to me and rests his hand on my back. "No, that's not it at all. Baby, I'm saying the idea of loving someone terrifies me. I never thought I could do it, but I already did. The moment I saw you rolling around on the floor at Peter's bachelor party, I realized something."

I glance up at him through wet lashes. "What?"

His touch is tender as he tells me, "You had my heart from the beginning. I thought it was gone, but you'd stolen it and kept it all this time. I love you, Cass. I'm going to find a way to be with you, in a way that you adore—a way that makes you feel good. There won't be any reason to cry." He leans in and presses his lips to my cheek and kisses away my tears.

CHAPTER 22
JON

We walk the deck after that, her hand in mine, fingers knitted together. The stars blink against the inky sky and the dark water is still as glass around the yacht. I don't deserve her. I know I don't. Regardless, I'm elated she finally confided in me, and I want to feel like this forever.

The concept of gentle sex crosses my mind. I don't know how to be that kind of lover. I've never tried. I focus on getting harder and higher—and taking the girl with me. That won't work for Cassie. I need to figure out what will, because I'm not letting her live like a chaste hermit, afraid of her own body.

I know Logan's friend can help her. In our conversation, she explained the way the human body tenses to defend itself. Rape victims can get stuck with their muscles stiff for years. Imagine holding your hand in a fist for an hour. It fucking hurts. Now think what that does to a body after years of being stuck that way. Her core might be stuck like that, playing defense even though there's no threat from me. Scars can feel painful, too. Most people don't notice them, but others wince with the slightest caress. Touching Cassie intimately can bring back a slew of emotions I never want her to feel again.

It doesn't mean no sex forever.

It means a lot of patience and even more time.

That conversation with Logan's friend was one of the most uncomfortable situations I've ever experienced. She described the female response to rape to explain the male response. I cut off the conversation there, and she never spoke of it again. At the time I wished it hadn't happened, but now I'm glad it did. I wouldn't have recognized how to help Cassie without it.

We stop at the railing and look out at the sea. Cassie leans on the metal bars while lifting my hand. She traces a circle on the back of my wrist, smiling softly as she does. "Do you remember kissing me here?"

Her touch is light, perfect. My voice hitches when I speak. "I could never forget that."

Her dark eyes shift to the side and glance at me before lifting my wrist to her lips. The heat of her mouth and brush of her tongue against my skin makes my heart beat harder. She steals my breath and inspires an instant response below my belt. I shift my stance, giving my growing girth more room.

Cassie continues to kiss me there, slowly dragging her mouth over my skin, licking, teasing, and kissing me there. I'm out of my element. I don't know what to do, what's next after sucking off a wrist. Do you go for an ankle? This is so fucking weird.

I scold myself. I'm thinking too much. The object is to make her feel loved and desired, while being very careful not to make her come hard. It's the opposite of everything I've always done. I can't go from her lips to her tits, and do my magic hands on her pussy. It'll hurt her, and I want her to feel good.

Cassie pulls away and looks up at me. "When do we need to be back?"

I can't think. Her voice shoots straight to my groin, and I'm annoyed that I'm such a dick. Why can't I focus on her? I can usually turn it on and off, but not with her. I stay that way, craving her kiss, wanting her touch, and any other form of affection she'll toss my way.

"Whenever we want."

A smile slips across her face. "Really?"

"Yeah, why?"

"Can we stay out here overnight?"

"If you'd like. There are beds below."

She presses her lips together and points to a spot on deck. "Can we bring some of the blankets up here? Maybe lay down, look at the stars, and pick up where we left off all those years ago?" Her wide brown eyes are locked on mine so intently that I can see the flecks of gold around her irises. Those dark lashes lower and then open again, shyly.

I'm careful. I want to bound around the deck, whooping with glee, but I keep my voice level, "If you want."

"I do."

I don't know what to tell her. How can I seduce a woman when I'm afraid I'll cause her pain? I drop my gaze to the deck. Staring at the wooden planks, I confess, "I don't know how to do this, Cassie. What if I hurt you?"

She takes my hands in hers and rises on her toes. "I'll tell you if it hurts, and you'll do something else. And if I do something you don't like, for any reason, you'll let me know so that I can try something else."

That sounds really good, perfect even, but there's one thing that bothers me, and if it's in my head I know it's in hers. "I don't want to sound like a prick, but what about you being married and your ideas about sex? That it's for marriage? Stolen kisses and things that don't belong to me? Cassie, baby, I'd be content just being your friend, if that's what you wanted."

She looks up at me from under those dark lashes and squeezes my hands. "I can't handle you as a friend. I want you too much. Those feelings aren't dead. They're still there. My affection for you isn't platonic, so while you might be okay being friends and only friends, I'm not. I don't want you with other girls. I want you for myself, and I don't want to share."

It feels like I'm walking through a battlefield with no armor every time she talks about us. I want her to tell me the truth and not hold back. I keep expecting her to walk away, but she doesn't.

I let out a sigh of relief and run my hand through my hair. "Thank God." My brow lifts and I look at her, offering a suave smile. "I was totally lying. I want you, too, more than you could possibly know."

Her giggle is light, and the way she looks at me says it all. "So, what do we do?"

"We figure it out."

CHAPTER 23
JON

I've never done anything like this before. Usually, if I want to be with a woman, I don't have to figure things out. But this is different. It's like completely starting over. I admit Monica screwed with my head so badly I didn't feel the need to learn anything. The first few girls I was with—women of my own choosing—were floored by me. It's not just the size of the package, although mine is far from standard equipment, it's how you use it. I could make a woman tense, purr, and beg for it. She'd arch her back and press into me willingly. I don't know what to do when the goal is to have 'nice' sex. That's not a thing, is it? How can it be anything but passionless and boring?

I need to fucking figure it out. What else can it be? How can I be with her without regressing, without hurting her? That fucker left a scar inside her body, a reminder of what he did. It's something that will always haunt her. I don't want to ignite those memories. I honestly have no goddamned clue what to do, how to love her.

I just know I'm not leaving. I won't give up, not if she wants this too.

We bring up blankets from below and make a pallet on the deck. Cassie leans back and pats the spot next to her. I kick off my shoes and lower myself until I'm next to her, sitting on the mounds of bedcovers.

There's only one thought in my mind, one thing that she can probably do and might enjoy. "What if I hold you, and we look up at the sky for a bit?"

Her head bobs up and down, making her curls sway. She tucks her long strands behind her ear and answers. "That sounds nice."

I cringe inwardly. 'Nice.' I hate that word.

'Your dick is nice.'

'You're a nice guy.'

'Your fucking abilities are nice.'

No guy ever whooped with glee because his woman thinks it was 'nice.' I groan inwardly wondering how to be more than that when everything is reduced to niceties.

It's nice or nothing.

I think she can read my mind because as soon as she rests her head on my chest, she splays her fingers across my stomach, and says, "I know this isn't what you wanted."

"Cass, that's not it at all." I hold her hand, trying to help her understand. "I don't know what to do. How are we supposed to be lovers when there's no fucking?"

I feel her shrug against me. "I'm not sure, but it probably has something to do with soft kisses and pulse points. This guy told me a long time ago that pulse point kisses are incredibly erotic. He was right. They are."

I play with a curl as she speaks. That feels like a lifetime ago. "I made that up."

She lifts her head, looks at me. "Really?"

"Pretty much."

She rolls toward me and places her arms on my chest and rests that cute chin on her open palms. "Then why the wrist? You could have picked someplace else."

My brows lift, and I shoot her a look that says it couldn't have been anywhere else. "You wouldn't have allowed me to kiss you here," I touch the side of her neck and sweep my finger across her shoulder. "Or any other usual spot, so I went for the wrist."

"I saw that in a movie once, before you did it, and thought it was silly—that it couldn't possibly feel like anything wonderful."

"And now, what do you think?"

"It's bliss. It's lightness and hope mixing, making me feel like I could do anything with you."

I lose myself in her gaze for a while, wanting to tell her how much she means to me, but I don't speak. From the look on her face, she knows. She figured out how messed up I am, and she still wants me.

Without glancing away, I lift her hand and press a light kiss on her wrist. She sighs contently, watching me as I adore her taste, flicking my tongue against her skin. I inhale deeply, enjoying her scent as my lips move across her flesh. I don't stay on the pulse point this time. I slowly wrap kisses around her wrist, like a bracelet and when I stop, she takes my hand and copies me.

It's a different kind of sensation, the lightness of it. There are no nails biting into me, nothing to make me scream out. Instead, her touch is a tender caress leaving me breathless and wondering if it's possible to be with someone so softly. I've only known sex in a way that mingles pain and pleasure. I thought this gentle stuff was for the passionless bastards who couldn't get laid.

But with her lips on me like that, I want more. I want the lightness of it to envelop me and fill me up inside. I want to hear Cassie moan with a content smile on her face instead of ripping her nails into my back. I don't want her teeth on my dick, either. I want her lips there, soft, gently pulling me into her mouth. I want to feel her swallow and see her smile up at me.

But there's more, more images flashing inside my mind of ways to touch her, places to hold. I can see myself gliding my hand over her thigh and pressing my lips to the curve of her lower back. I want to press my face against her there, kneel and hold her. I want to feel my skin on hers, warm and wonderful.

I'm quiet too long, and neither of us moves until Cassie says, "What are you thinking about?"

"I'm thinking I'm completely fucked up and so lucky to have you." She runs her fingers along my brow, trailing the pads of her fingers around to my temple and then tangling them in my hair. I'm lost in her eyes, staring at the flecks of gold that come alive when she's happy.

"Most guys would say that you chose the wrong word. I'm a walking oxymoron, a living breathing dichotomy. I strip by night and am a sexless prude by day."

"No, you're not, baby. You're the most sensual, beautiful woman I've ever seen. Your scars are deep, and come all the way to the surface. Most people hide all that, but you don't. It makes you stronger and more gorgeous than you could possibly imagine."

My eyes flick between her lips and eyes as I speak. She has no idea how beautiful she is, how strong. "Kiss me, Cass?"

It's a question and an honest-to-God plea. I want her lips on mine so badly I'm ready to crawl over and climb on top of her. That's not what she needs. I remain on my back, and stick to tender touches and thoughts.

Cassie's gaze dips to my lips. She pushes up on her elbows as she dips her head, and presses her lips to my mouth. They're so soft, so full, so perfect. I want to devour her. I want to drink her in and never stop. I feel the sweep of her tongue brushing wet and warm against my lips. I open and let her in, enjoying the sensation of her mouth on mine.

I fell in love with a woman that I never kissed until years later, and now that she's here in my arms, her body pressed against mine, I feel like I could fly. Every inch of my body is humming as if I've been smacked with an electric charge. I want to sing at the top of my lungs and tell every bastard out there she's mine, and I'm fucking lucky to have her.

Cassie Hale is finally mine.

She pulls back, breaks the kiss. A coy grin flirts with her lips. "Your lips disappear when you smile, Jon Ferro."

"I can't help it. You're here. You're kissing me. You love me." It feels strange to be so brutally honest, to let it all out there, but I'm not afraid of admitting it. She makes me a better man, she always has. I'm not one of those shits who doesn't know how good he has it. I know more than anyone that I don't deserve her, that she's so much better than me.

She shifts her weight, swings a leg, perches over me and asks, "May I?"

Fuck, she wants to sit on me? I nod, wide-eyed, and hope I can control myself. I tuck my hands behind my head and swallow hard as she straddles me. Even with clothing on, I can feel the heat between her legs radiating through my jeans. If I wasn't completely hard before, I am now.

Cassie perches above me, her body surrounded by stars and moonlight. She shifts her weight causing me to suck in sharply. I knot my fingers behind my head and look up at her. The way her dress clings to the bottoms of her breasts is hypnotic. I could watch her forever. The heat of her body, the way she acts like she has no clue, and the gentle breeze in her hair, lifting each curl off her shoulders reminds me of a fairytale long forgotten.

The word she chose before was accurate—this is bliss.

Cassie lowers her body and presses it to mine. Her tits are soft and warm, squeezing into me, stealing my sanity. I don't want her to emotionally detach from me. I know she could, so I won't pressure her. She's setting the pace, choosing what we do and when. For once, sex isn't about getting off. It's about the other person, about making her feel loved and cherished. There's an intuitive part to it, things I feel pulled to do that Cass would like, but I don't trust myself. I don't want her walls to dart up. I want her in the moment with me.

Her lips are by my ear, her breath spilling down my neck. "What are you thinking?"

I'm thinking I'm going to fuck this up. That when you realize I have as much emotional shit to lug behind me as Sean does, you'll run and never look back. People expect his baggage. His fall from grace was horrifically public, but no one knows what happened to me.

I find my voice and manage, "That you make me feel things I've not felt before. I don't know what to act on, what to ignore." I'm breathing hard, and I'm too hot, even though the breeze is cool.

She runs her nails along my temple, pushing my hair away from my face. She keeps her nose nuzzled to my ear. "Like what?"

"Cass, I don't think I should."

"Jonathan..."

The way she says my name is the materialization of seduction. It rolls off her tongue in a velvety sound from the back of her throat. Combined with that breathy voice, it's completely erotic and shoots straight below the belt. She could purr to me like that all night, and I'm pretty sure I'd come from that alone.

"Yeah, baby?"

"I don't think we should hold back. We should tell each other, and ask if it sounds good. Ask me if I want it?"

My mouth goes dry, and I swallow hard. The talk alone is going to undo me. I feel her pull back until I see her dark eyes above me. Maybe I appear indifferent, and I don't want her to think that.

I tell her the truth. "I have my hands behind my head because I want to touch you. I want to put them under your shirt and feel your skin. I want to be with you, Cass. I want to know what it feels like to slide my palms up to your sides and feel the weight of your breasts in my hands. I want to kiss you deeply and lose myself in your arms, inside your body, but I don't trust myself with this. I'm afraid we'll get caught in the moment, and I don't want to hurt you. I don't ever want to cause you pain of any kind, ever again."

Her chin lowers to her chest as she watches me. That soft, dark hair hangs over her shoulders, and there's a rim of pale light illuminating her slim form. I want to touch her face, trail my fingers along her skin. I want to learn every inch of her, taste every part, and miss nothing.

Cassie's dark eyes try to hold mine, but I look away. It's too much, and this isn't a good idea. There's too much risk for her. I'm not worth it. I pull my hands out from behind my head, intending to put them on her hips to move her off of me, but she reaches out for them and pins them over my head.

"Cass." I don't look at her.

"Jonathan."

"This isn't going to work."

"How do you know? You barely tried."

"It's just not." I yank my hands down, but she leans forward and places all of her weight on them. Her thighs inadvertently squeeze me, trying to keep me still.

"Jon, I want to try."

"I don't." The words are clipped, and I expect them to sting enough to startle her into letting me up.

Instead, she gets pissed. She leans within an inch of my nose and growls in my face. "Yes, you do, and I'm not going to let you treat me like damaged goods. If you want to be with me, do it. If you don't want me, say it." She's glaring at me, hurt plainly visible on her face.

"That's not it."

"Then what is it?"

"Cassie, I don't want to say it—"

"It's okay. I get it. It's me. I'm not worth the bother. I already know it, so just admit it!" Her strained voice warbles as it comes out.

She's near tears and won't listen. She rushes on, blaming herself as she rolls off of me and gets to her knees. She's about to stand when I grab her hands. She doesn't look at me, so I tug her arms. She still won't look at me, so I take her face in my hands and hold it between my palms. I want her to hear me.

"Cass, that couldn't be farther from the truth."

Her eyes won't meet mine. "I know what I am."

"No, you don't. You act like you're the one no one should want, but that's not it. I love you. I always will."

She carefully looks up at me from underneath those wet lashes that blinked back tears. "Then why?"

"Because I'm not worth the risk. This," I drop my hands and gesture between us, "could hurt you. I can't promise I won't, and I won't even know until it's too late. I can't risk hurting you."

There's a dead silence between us. Her face drops and sadness fills her eyes. She pulls away from me and lowers that perfect ass to her feet, kneeling on the deck in a pile of blankets. I mirror her, waiting for her to say something, but she's silent. I made it worse.

After a few moments, she asks, "Do you love me?"

"You know I do."

"Then you need to trust me, Jon. I don't think we'll figure it out on the first try. We may never get to a point where I'm okay with everything, but I don't want you to shirk away because you're afraid."

"It's not worth it." I'm not worth it.

She takes my face in her hands, rubs her thumbs along my cheeks just above the jaw. She hears me loud and clear. "You are worth it. You mean everything to me, and if it takes stumbling around in bed with you to figure it out, I will. If days turn into months and months turn into years, I'm not giving up. Loving you isn't optional. I can't stop, and it will be really embarrassing if I keep pawing at you day in and day out, and you keep saying no."

I move, reach for her hands and smooth mine over hers, and then lose myself in her eyes. She's so hopeful, so perfectly gorgeous that I want to have faith this will work out too. "What if I accidentally hurt you?"

"I'll tell you."

"Are you sure, Cass?"

"I've never been more certain of anything in my entire life." She doesn't fight fair.

The woman stops using words and switches to a more deadly weapon—that mouth. Those lips land on my jaw, and she kisses a path from my chin to my neck. The feeling of her soft skin on mine makes me light-headed. I want to sway back and pull her down with me, but I manage to stay upright. Her teeth graze my jaw, and I suck in a jagged breath.

She lifts her head, eyeing me. "You don't like that, do you?"

No one has ever asked me that before. I've made the same movement too many times, and it usually just makes the woman do it again. Cass can tell the difference.

"Not really. It reminds me of someone I'd rather forget." Monica. I don't have to say her name, Cass knows.

She nods slowly, leans in and licks the skin just below the base of my neck. The reaction is nearly identical. I suck in a jagged breath and stiffen. "You like that, though, right?"

She's sitting on her feet, watching me. She's stripped my defenses. I'm completely vulnerable, and she knows it. I nod once, not trusting my voice. Cassie reaches for me and does it again. I make the same sound. Her hands slip under my shirt, and I feel her nails on my back, ready to dig in. She doesn't do it the same way. Instead of drawing blood and marking me like a fucking animal, her touch is light. I exhale a shaky breath, unexpectedly.

I hear a content sound in my ear, like she can tell what I like and what I don't. A moment later she's tugging my shirt over my head and pushing me down on the blankets. Her fingers spread across my chest, and I watch her do it. She lingers above me, her eyes sweeping over my body.

"I want to touch you everywhere, in every way. I want to figure out what you like, and where you like it. May I?" Soft brown curls surround her face as she gazes down at me. Her chest swells as she breathes and there's a softness in her eyes that is hard to look away from.

"I'd love that."

CHAPTER 24
CASSIE

His voice is barely a whisper. His nerves are palpable, and I know he's desperate to avoid more regret. I never thought he'd blame himself for what happened to me or think he wasn't worth the danger of what might happen. He's worth risking everything. He always has been. He saved me more than once, in every way.

STRIPPED 2

His body is perfect in the dim light. The blankets beneath his skin are inky like the ocean. Moonlight spills across his ripped chest and muscular abs, revealing every line.

I place my hand on his neck and trail the pads of my fingers down slowly, tracing the lines of his chest, passing over his taut nipple, and then touching further below. His skin is smooth and warm, his body firm with every muscle corded tight like he's trying to hold back.

I lean in and press my lips to his ear, whispering, "Relax, Jon."

His body shivers and tenses before I see him unwind. His fingers uncurl, and he closes his eyes. I watch his chest rise and fall for a moment, holding my hand on his flat stomach before sweeping my touch to his side. I trace the lines that disappear beneath his waistband, then pull his shoulder to roll him over. Once he's face down I look at his back.

I hesitate to touch the scars, but I want to. When I finally reach out, he looks back at me. I stop, frozen, waiting for him to tell me not to do it.

Jon says, "I think I understand."

I pull my hand back and hold it close to my heart. "Understand what?"

"Why you're willing to endure the pain to be with me. Why it's worth it."

I stare at him, unable to speak, heart pounding in my chest. These aren't things I talk about—not with anyone.

"Cass, I'm not you, and I'll never fully know what you've been through, but my closest experience would be getting sliced with shrapnel. Given the chance, I'd never exchange that day for anything. I'd do the same thing every time and live with the scars because it was the first day I got close to you. I wanted you to trust me so badly."

My voice is a whisper, "I know."

"You wouldn't even go out with me, not as friends or anything. I realized how much

I loved you that day, how I'd do anything for you. I'd dive into that explosion all over again if it made you realize how much I love you. It's not something you'd ever ask, but all the same, you couldn't stop me." He quiets for a moment. Jon's lying on his side, head propped up slightly with his hand, waiting for me to affirm what he's said.

I press my lips together and nod, unable to speak. He's watching me from the covers, sitting lower than me, spread out like a bronzed god on the deck looking up at me with that beautiful face. The corner of his mouth lifts into a slight smile as he reaches out and touches my hand with his finger.

"You're right," I say. "It's not that different. I want my life to be a certain way, despite what's happened. I won't stop living because of it. I won't give up. These scars," I reach for him, touch my finger to his back, to one of the raised welts, "marred you forever, but to me, they make you more beautiful. I can still see your face in my mind, the way you helped everyone, not caring about yourself. That was the first time I saw the genuine Jonathan Ferro. Every time I see these scars, it reminds me that man is in this body. When it comes down to it, you'll fight to save the people around you."

His face lights up with humble satisfaction. I see him, even through all that bravado. The next part is hard to say, but I plow through it. He needs to know.

"Save me, Jon. Figure things out with me. Be an awkward lover with me so we can get to whatever comes after that." I'm well aware of how hot my face feels, how red I must be. My hands are on his arm, sliding up and down, tracing the muscles corded tight beneath his skin.

This man has no idea his heart is vulnerable, raw. He's driven to save everyone except himself. That's the way he's been since I met him, but I don't think either of us realized it then. I didn't see it until the day of Jack Gray's exhibit at the museum. I was a fool and nearly lost the best man I've ever met in my entire life because I assumed I knew everything. I was wrong. I knew nothing about him. But today is different. He's kind and compassionate, to a fault. He'd give a stranger the shirt off his back and not ask a single question. That smile covers a multitude of scars, and his laugh masks the pain flowing through memories I wish I could take away.

Jon's eyes lift and meet mine. The way he looks at me makes me want to lean in and kiss him. We stay like that for a moment before he lies down again, and I continue tracing the rises and falls of his body across his muscular shoulders and down to his waist.

I slant toward him and place a kiss on the small of his back, lingering there for a moment. I want to press my cheek to his back and hold him, but I don't. Not right now.

My curls brush across his skin when I sit up. I notice his happy shiver, the same as before. He likes that sensation, so I lean forward and do it again. My hair lightly touching his skin, grazing over it in a light caress. He moans my name in response.

I reach for his arm and roll him over to face me. When I do, Jon looks up, his face a combination of adoration and longing. I lean down until my lips are almost to his and smile. I pull away without giving him the kiss he thought he was getting, and drag the tips of my curls over his washboard stomach. I follow it by doing the same thing with the tips of my fingers, barely touching his skin, and feeling him draw in jagged breaths as I pass over his body.

I tug my dress over my head and toss it aside. As my hands reach up for my bra, I say, "It's my turn."

His eyes open, flashing with emotion. I toss the lingerie aside and sit there for a moment. The wind blows my hair over my shoulder, covering me. Jon sits up slowly. There's so much conflict on his face that I wonder if he'll do it. He reaches out and lets his hand hover in the air for so long I think he'll say no, but he finally lowers his palm to my shoulder. His strong hand strokes my skin, jarring memories I wish I could banish. It would help hold them at bay if he spoke, if he used his voice to keep me in the present.

I tell him so. "Please talk to me. I need to hear your voice."

Jon begins to describe what he wants to do to me. His lips sweep my neck, whispering into my ear, "I want to feel every inch of you beneath my hands. I love your soft skin and your scent. God, Cassie... You light me up and steal my breath. You make me whole in a way I thought I'd never be." He leans in, touching his lips to my shoulder. "I've wanted to kiss this spot since I met you."

He begins trailing his perfect lips over my skin and retelling our story, kiss by kiss. He doesn't touch my breasts until he's caressed and kissed every inch of my back, shoulders, and down to my waist. At some point, they're the only part he hasn't touched.

Jon hesitates, looking at the mounds of soft flesh as I lie back in the blankets. I take his hands in mine and place them on my waist. "I wanted you to do this once before."

"I remember." He seems afraid, timid. The wind blows his hair gently, reminding me of the arrogant boy who used to look out at me from behind those eyes, of innocence lost. Despite that, the man who's above me now is so much better than he realizes. Jon is stronger, kinder, and better despite all of it.

"You won't ruin me." I tangle my hands in his hair on the side of his head for a moment, enjoying the sensation. "I won't blame you for seducing me."

"Me?" he laughs and sounds truly happy. "You seduced me, fully, completely. I'd die happy right now, and I've barely touched you."

I place my hands over his and move them slowly up my sides. I feel him hesitate during their ascent. "Then touch me. I want you to feel me, all of me."

He nods slowly, the movement making his dark hair fall into his blue eyes. He doesn't push it away. Instead, I take my hands away, and he slides his palms over me. His hands feel warm and strong against my skin. I place my hands over my head and watch him.

After cupping me, he draws back and moves. He's lying on his side, looking down at me, tracing my curves with his finger. He circles my breast from base to tip, before doing the same to the other side. I don't think ahead, and I don't think back. I'm here, now, with him, and I realize I still want more. I've never had anyone treat me like this before. I feel cherished. It's not fucking, and he's not using me. Love and adoration motivate his actions. His fingers trace me, touching me lighting over and over again making the warmth in my belly coil tighter, and want more than skin on skin.

I tangle my hands in his hair and breathe, "Kiss me."

When his lips come down on mine, I arch my back, pressing my chest against his firm body. As our tongues tangle together, the heat I've been feeling finally starts touching forbidden places.

I feel alive. I don't want to hide from him. I want all of me against all of him. I want his hands on me, his lips tasting me, and I want him inside of me.

I reach for his pants and undo the button, followed by the zipper. I slip them off along with his boxers and wrap my hand around his hard length. It's so warm and perfect in my hand. I close my palm around him and move my wrist in a way that makes him moan.

I watch his body writhe, and those narrow hips buck into my hand with a controlled rhythm. There's an expression on his face I've never seen before. As I continue to work him, sliding my hand up and down over his shaft, I watch how he reacts. His lips part and he's completely relaxed. His guard is down with no walls in sight. He trusts me completely, and I find I'm almost jealous. I don't know how to do that.

His eyes flick open and he shifts, pushing me to the bottom and breathing harder than before. "You'll make me come if you keep doing that."

"That's the idea, isn't it?" I smile, and he presses a kiss to my nose.

"Yes, but not yet. Can I touch you, Cassie? Do you want me to?" He lingers there, studying me. His hand is at my waist, above my panties. He's waiting for me to say yes. He won't move unless I say he can. It's strange having a man want to do things to me to make me feel good.

I slip my hand over his and lower it. It lowers beneath my waistline, and he rests his palm there just above the place that's warm and ready for his touch. In the back of my mind, warnings bells start to chime:

It'll hurt. You'll cry. He'll leave. Don't do this. You can't survive the rejection—

I silence the worries by pulling his mouth down onto mine. I get lost in the kiss and let it fill my head. Soon my hips are swaying, lifting toward his hand, and I hear my voice making noises I don't make. But it's me.

My eyes flutter between open and closed before Jon's hand slips between my lower lips very carefully. He strokes me, pressing a single finger against my core and sweeping upward toward my belly. His eyes bore into mine as he does it making me feel exposed, completely raw. In response, my heart pounds harder, and my past nightmares rear their ugly heads.

They grab my throat hard, and I nearly start crying. "Talk to me, Jon. Say something and don't stop. I need to hear your voice."

Jon stills his hand. "Of course, I shouldn't have stopped telling you how much I love you. How much I want you. Cassie, you make me feel things I've never felt before. You've put this massive amount of hope inside me, and I'm worried it's going to explode. I have a cheesy smile on my face that won't go away. This voice I'm speaking with is cheerful. Cassie, I've never been happy, I mean truly elated before, and certainly not for this long. It's because of you. It's because of your smile, and your touch. It's from your kiss and your caress." He continues to speak and at some point, his hand begins to move again.

His fingers stay outside, cupping me, gently passing over my lips until my eyes close and I relax fully. His words feel like a song chasing away the demons. It's just us. As he whispers in my ear, his finger slips inside, past my seam, pressing against that sensitive spot. He stays still for a moment, allowing me to adjust to the sensation.

His lips press against my cheek for a moment, before he says, "Tell me what you want."

My eyes flick open, and I look at him.

A sheepish look crosses his face. "I'm sorry, I can't tell if this is hellish or if you like it. You're all scrunched up, and too quiet. I can stop."

"I don't want you to stop."

"Please tell me you're not going to insist on doing this, even if it makes you sick and causes you pain." He begins to pull his hand away, but I place mine over it and stop him.

"That's not it. I haven't done anything like this. Well, I've done this, just not this way. I like your hands on me. I'm wondering if I'll like more, what it'll feel like."

"Do you want me to slip my finger all the way inside, Cass?"

I nod.

He shakes his head, "I'm not risking anything unless I hear your voice. You have to say it, baby. Tell me what you want. Tell me what to do, how hard, and when to stop." He's watching me closely.

Worry pinches the corners of his eyes, and I know sex is going to need to be like this for a while. He doesn't trust himself, and I don't know where my line is, or if there is one. Part of it depends on what Jon does and how he does it.

Watching his eyes, I tell him, "I want it."

"What do you want?"

"I want you to rub me, the way you were, gently. I liked that." I feel so strange saying this out loud. I'd rather drink Drano than play this weird version of truth or dare.

The awkwardness doesn't last long, though. I'm wet, and the way Jon moves his finger over me is too arousing to ignore. I tip my head back, close my eyes, and let my hands fall to my side.

"Cassie, you can't do that." His hand slows. I moan, holding onto it. "Stay with me. Tell me when to stop and what to do. I'd love it if I knew exactly what to do, but I don't. You have to tell me what you want."

I look up into his face and want to kiss him. "I love you," I say.

He smiles boyishly. "I love you, too."

"Do you think it feels the same?" He doesn't understand so I elaborate. "This, you touching me, compared to the way I was touching you."

He grins. "I'm not sure. Do you like it?"

I nod and remember to speak. "Yes, I like it a lot. I want you to slip a finger inside of me." My hand is on his arm, almost like I don't want him to, as if I'm holding him back.

"Are you sure?" He glances at it too. "There's plenty of time, Cassie."

I squeeze his forearm. "I want to know if it feels good or if it makes me want to cry. I want to know."

Jon nods and his gaze drops with grief. The only way to find out if he'll hurt me is to do it. Jon swallows hard and the lump on his throat bobs. He sweeps his finger gently over me once, then again, before placing it just above my core. His eyes lock on mine, and I don't mean to, but my hand is on his arm again, ready to make him stop.

"Tell me." His voice is gentle, careful. "I won't know if you don't say anything."

I nod and force myself to speak even though my voice is tight, even though panic is racing through my body, ready to rip me in half. "I'll tell you. I'm nervous, that's all. Nothing hurt up to this point and hearing your voice helps keep my mind out of the past. I like it when you talk to me." I smile nervously at him.

Jon smiles back. "I love talking to you. And I know this is hard. It's difficult for me as well, Cass. I've wanted you for so long and now that I can have you, well, I don't want this to be clinical, but I think it has to be right now."

I nearly choke on a laugh. "This isn't how gynecological visits go, Jon. If they did, every doctor in the city would have a line from here to Jersey with eager women waiting for appointments. It's not clinical," I assure him, "but it is different. Will you pet me for a moment, and then try?"

He nods thoughtfully, keeping those sapphire eyes locked on mine. As his hand moves against me, I feel the tension fade away. He says sweet things in my ear, his warm breath washing across my face as he runs his gentle touch between my lower lips. My eyelids feel heavy until he slips his finger inside. I stiffen and yelp, my spine going ramrod straight.

He immediately tries to pull back, but I stop him. "It doesn't hurt. I just..." My heart feels like it's going to explode. Regret gives way to relief, and I start crying.

Jon pulls his hand away and cradles me in his arms. He's crooning in my ear, apologizing. "It'll be all right, baby. I've got you. Nothing will hurt you." He kisses my head and continues saying comforting things as I shiver in his arms.

I don't understand. My body reacted wrong. My mind was okay with it. The long scar inside me didn't make me want to puke. Jon's hand felt good. Then with a single touch, everything changed and I'm a shaking blubbering mess.

Jon wipes the tears away and kisses my cheek as he holds me tight. I rest my head against his chest and stare out at the sea.

I don't know how to fix this. At one time this didn't happen to me. I thought if I loved Jon things would be okay, that we could work it out. I never thought my mind might rewire itself over the years, but it must have. It's like my body bypassed my brain. That tender touch shorted me out, and I feel like he did the same thing as Mark.

That's why the tears fall.

That's why I can't stop them.

I know Jon won't let me try this more than a few times. It hurts him, too. It's too much to ask anyone, especially since I'm not convinced getting through this is even possible. I always thought that one day, with the right guy, I'd cross the lake of torment and land on the other side. There's one question burning my tongue, one thought I'm too afraid to ask.

What if there is no other side?

CHAPTER 25
CASSIE

Last night was difficult. This morning I feel like I've been dowsed, drowned, and wrung out emotionally. Jon is headed to a rehearsal for the wedding, but he's nervous about leaving me. After a long night of tears and tenderness, he called that doctor. She said she could see me today, and talk about options. I don't want to get my hopes up. I'm not sure what choices are even available. I mean, it's not like we can pretend it never happened. The things Mark did will always be there. The scars won't vanish, no matter how loudly I command them to go.

I'm sitting on the couch and staring at the little picture of the Seine River. Beth plops down next to me, admiring the new design on her glittery pink cast. "So, Jon hasn't let me strip since this happened." She taps on her cast. "Did you know he had contractors in there yesterday?"

"He did?" I blink at her. "Doing what?"

"They measured everything, and pulled out a lot of that old paneling. Some walls are entirely bare now. Other walls are gone, and the stage is getting a facelift—new floors and these soft velvet curtains. I got chased out before I could figure out what they were doing. Want to know the weirdest part?"

"Yeah."

"No one worked yesterday or the day before, and the Club didn't open last night. It's closed tomorrow too."

I glance at her, wondering what Jon's doing. He's not said anything about it. "Do you think he's just updating aesthetics?"

She shakes her head. "No, it seems like he's changing the place up. It doesn't look like a strip club anymore. When I went by last night, they were hanging light fixtures and putting in these cool looking leather benches and booths. He added more club chairs and tables along the front of the stage, but you have to see it. Guys sitting there can't reach us anymore to hand us cash. I'm not sure what he's doing."

That must be why we went out last night. He didn't want me to see. I can't believe he'd close the place after everything I told him about how much these girls need their jobs. There's been very little fighting, and most of my friends are excited to work since Jon took over.

"He didn't say anything to me." I stare at the wall, thinking.

Beth leans in next to me with big eyes and bumps her shoulder to mine. Her fingers are intertwined and clasped tightly, arms straight, and elbows locked. As she sways toward me, her arms go the other way, like a pendulum. "So, what's new?"

I turn to her. "Nothing. Why?"

Her lips have a strange curve. It's like she shoved an orange in her mouth and it doesn't fit. Beth drops her hands and sighs dramatically. "You are such a liar. Come on, spill. I've been so good not prying, but the guy is a Ferro, and he's been sleeping on your floor, and—Cassie what's wrong?"

My bottom lip juts out. I wish I could just swallow my head. I don't want to talk about it, but there's no way Beth will leave it alone now. "Nothing."

"I'm going to kill him. I mean, your dickhead husband is a piece of shit, but if I'd known Jon was—"

I cut her off. "Jon's not like that! He's been perfect."

"Then why the tears?"

I glance over at her through glassy eyes. The world is distorted, blurry, and sad. I have the perfect guy, but I can't be with him. I figure out how to say it, and tell her what happened. I tell her about Mark and the long periods of time where he used and hurt me, filling in things I'd left out previously. Beth knew Mark was a dick, but had no idea of the extent of his abuse.

I finish by telling her about Jon, and how he's supported me. By the time I'm at the end of the story, tears are rolling down my cheeks, and my voice is flat. I feel dead inside. It's a story I'd rather not tell, something I don't want anyone to know. I want to be normal. I want to feel normal. I don't want this heavy part of my past looming over me forever, but every time I nearly pass it, it comes back stronger.

I swallow hard and clear my throat. "Apparently there's a doctor that can help me, but I really don't want to go."

"I can understand why you wouldn't. But Cassie, OMG, Jon hasn't left your side. He loves you!" She presses her palms together, giddy. "The guy said he'd wait for you."

"I think he'd wait forever. We'll be asexual old people, and he'll turn into my brother. Then my mom can adopt him and love him more than she loves me."

I'm not acting rational, and I know it. It feels like I'm caught in a freefall and I'm about to hit the bottom. I have everything I wanted, even snagged the guy, but there's no future for us. No kids. No pleasure. No passion. Nausea heats in my stomach and washes over me in a wave. I press my hand over my mouth and wish I had a mint.

"Your mom is a piece of work. I won't say anything about that. Your brother is a dick. And Jon is the guy who got away, right? He's here now, and he's not leaving. At first, I was pissed he hung around so long, but with Kam's guys across the street, a Ferro on the floor seemed like a good move."

"Plus he bought you glitter tape."

She beams at her pink cast. "There was that. Can I ask a stupid question?"

"Go ahead."

"What's wrong with seeing the doctor and thinking about whatever she tells you? It's not like it can make things worse, right? I mean, you can't be with him, and you want to, so what do you have to lose?"

As her words sink in, I realize it's not about Jon or sex. It's about me facing my past, looking directly at it, assessing the damage done, and accepting it. I've never accepted what Mark did to me. I never told anyone he forced me, I rarely use the word rape. It's not that I don't know what it means, it's that I was stupid enough to let it happen to me. It wasn't a single occurrence, which makes me partially to blame. When I first met Jon, I thought I was strong. I thought I'd face life head on and shoulder my way past anything that tried to bring me down. I thought I'd fight back or die trying.

I didn't fight back. That's what bothers me. I never threw a punch. I never thought about hurting him while he slept. I could have done so many things, left so much sooner than I did—but I stayed. I convinced myself Mark's behavior was a fluke. I forgave it. I thought I was supposed to, and when I did, he treated me so wonderfully that I thought it was over. Mark gave me so much attention and affection that I felt like he couldn't live without me.

Then it'd happen again. The cycle would repeat. Anger. Rape. Sweetness. Presents and promises that never came to be. I shrunk back in my mind and cowered. I wouldn't have left if he hadn't scared me that last time. I didn't expect to see the sunrise again. He would have killed me, and I let it happen. All of it. I sank into this unending tide of misery, waiting for it to wash out again, but it never left.

My voice is a whisper. "Nothing. I have nothing else to lose, but I'm not sure if I can face it again, Beth."

She presses her hand over mine and squeezes. "Do you want Jon to go with you?"

I shake my head. "He already offered, but I don't think I can manage it in front of him. It's too much, you know?"

She nods. "I get it. Listen, how about this? I'll go with you. I'll go where you tell me. If you want me to stay in the waiting room, I will. If you want me to come with you, I can do that too. When stuff is this emotional, it's hard to think clearly. It might help to have someone there supporting you—even if it's awkward. I'm here for you Cassie. I'll go with you."

I nod slowly, trying not to cry. I never expected to find such a good friend, but I have. "I'd like that. Thanks, Beth."

CHAPTER 26
CASSIE

Beth sits next to me at the doctor's office, and when they call me back, I nod for her to come with me. We're in a women's health medical mall, and I'm well aware it looks like we're lesbians. Beth grins and puts her arm around my shoulders. "People are so stupid."

I shake her off. I'm too fried to deal with the weird stares. It's irrational to think they know what happened, that they're judging me, but that's what it feels like. "You can chide humanity on the way out. Not right now, okay?"

"Sorry, I was trying to make you laugh. I'll stop."

"Thanks."

We pass several doors, and a nurse leads me into a pale gray office with silver chairs in front of a glass desk. There's an empty white executive chair behind it. Bookcases line the walls from floor to ceiling. I pick a seat and sit down, folding my hands in my lap.

I didn't realize I'd be in an office. I thought she'd insist on an exam. Honestly, I've avoided the women's doctor since getting married. The thought of pap smears and annuals makes me sick if I think about it.

A tall, thin woman walks into the room. She stops, closes the door, and walks over to the desk with a computer tablet in her hand. She places it down and looks up at us. "I'm Doctor Bellamy. Which of you is Cassie Hale?"

I raise my hand like I'm in school. "Me."

She juts out a palm to shake. I take it and exchange pleasantries, but my mind is elsewhere. As she shakes Beth's hand, I realize it sounds like we're underwater. Voices echo strangely. My hands are on the arms of the chair, nails biting into the soft fabric. My heart is pounding like I'm going to get jumped by a bear.

I barely breathe, "I can't do this."

Dr. Bellamy nods. "It's all right. You can leave at any time, but may I tell you a few things before you go? It sometimes helps to know what we do, how we can help."

I pause. "I don't have to tell you what happened?"

"Not today. Jon gave me enough information." Her eyes sweep over me. "It's common to feel frightened and avoid coming to this kind of place, but it's where you'll find the most help."

She begins to explain that women's health is more than annual exams. It's about helping women from adolescence through old age with issues that affect our gender. She tells me that she gets referrals from other doctors and why they can't do it. Apparently this is a specialty area. I've never heard of this before, and I live in a major city.

I tell her that. "How come I've never heard of the other services offered? Like helping someone with my situation?"

"Well, unless you know someone who's been here or needed this type of care, it's not something people talk about at the dinner table. Or anywhere else. It's very personal and private." She's leaning against her desk, legs out in front of her with clunky black shoes sticking out from under gray slacks. She's at least twice Jon's age. Her silvery hair is tied at the base of her neck and pierced by a pencil.

Beth is quiet, listening carefully with her hands folded in her lap.

The doctors ask me some questions, and I don't see the relevance. Do I feel like I need to pee frequently? Yes. Do I get up a lot at night? Yes. Has it ever hurt to have sex? Yes. Even without abuse. It's always hurt. The questions stray the other way again, away from sex. She's asking about my day, what I do. She asks if I'm in danger now.

I shake my head. "No, Jon chased him off."

"How is Jonathan?" She watches me for a moment, and I can tell she's wondering if I know.

I glance at Beth, and she doesn't need a hint. She gets it. "I need to pee. Where's the ladies' room?" Dr. Bellamy points and Beth vacates the room.

A moment later, it's just the doctor and me. "Jon said you knew something happened to him."

"I suspected it. He was young at the time. Something like that can cause a young man a lot of misery later in life." Her eyes are hazel, with big flecks of gray the same shade as her hair.

"I shouldn't ask you about him."

"He gave me permission to tell you anything about him."

"Really?"

"Yes, Jonathan is good like that. He's a very caring person, and I know he feels like he had control of that situation so long ago, but he didn't. He was a kid. It wasn't his fault, and if anyone had known about it at the time, that woman would have been sent to jail. Sexual assault happens regardless of gender or age. I wish it didn't."

"Does he have this too?" I'm vague, but she understands my question.

"I don't know, but I'd think not. Women's bodies are built differently than men. The natural way we react to pain is to tighten and curve around the afflicted area. In your case, it's a part of the body that is surrounded by very strong muscles, which were probably already too tight. Add the stress of what happened, and trying to force the muscles open just hurt more. Think of it like any other muscle in your body. When it gets hurt, we cradle it, keep it close, and try to protect it. The muscle fibers surrounding the area shorten and become tight. It's painful when you force it to stretch. Some women are in pain without intercourse, as well. They constantly hurt and have no idea why. It could be from a trauma or surgery, they both cause a reaction that's hard to suppress."

"Then how do you fix it?"

"I want you to know that while we can make progress, for some people the pain never completely goes away. You'll have good days and bad days, and in the beginning, it's one step forward, two steps back. Does your scar make you feel nauseated? Without touching it?" Jon must have told her about that.

I nod. "Sometimes."

"Nausea, we can help. Scar tissue sometimes becomes tender and over sensitive. We can treat that in the office, or I can tell you how to do it. Was that the main issue last night?"

Tears form in my eyes, and I blink rapidly, trying to hold them back. "Yes, and it hurt a little. It didn't feel good."

She's patient with me and speaks kindly. I don't feel like she pities me, it's that she emphasizes, she knows how hard it is sometimes. Still, there's hopefulness in her voice I can't ignore. We talk a little longer and by the time I'm heading home, I feel more convinced the other side of this storm is real—which makes me more determined to get there.

CHAPTER 27
JON

I hate weddings. I used to love weddings. It was easy to find a hot girl and nail her, but I'm not interested now. I want to get home to Cassie.

I wanted to be there with her today, but between the rehearsal and her request for privacy, I came here. It's driving me fucking crazy to stand here with a smile on my face while Cassie is home crying her eyes out. I want to help her through this, but I know she has to see this through on her own. I can't fix her mind. I can't mend her body. I can only support her.

Which makes me want to rush out the doors. But Mr. Turkey, Sidney's pet vulture isn't cooperating. She's insisting the damn thing be in the ceremony. We're in a cathedral, and she brought God's most disgusting creature into a holy place. If I weren't in a rush to leave, it'd be hilarious to sit here and watch them try to figure it out.

But that's not the way today is, and when I see Uncle Luke's face, I want to smash my fist into his smug smile. He's sitting on a pew near the front next to my mother, who hasn't said two words to me since I arrived. She's pissed.

We practice walking down the long aisle at St. Pete's, pacing all the groomsmen and bridesmaids to reach the alter at the right time and make the most of it. Sidney would have preferred a backyard wedding.

Somehow mother convinced her to do a Ferro wedding, which means a big, lavish Italian wedding with tons of press.

Mother pretends the bird will be allowed in here on the wedding day, but there's no way in hell she'll actually follow through on that promise. I was born into a family of liars, willing to do anything to move their chess pieces across the board. Nothing is beyond these people. I'm ashamed to say they're family, but then I look at Pete and wonder—he's changed over the past few years. Since he met Sidney, he's not the womanizing manwhore he'd been before. And Sean, he's leaning against a column, arms folded across his chest, glaring. I can't forget what Avery said about him. Everyone wears a mask—only fools fail to see that. I can't write my brothers off, not yet. We were close once. Maybe it can be that way again.

Before I have time to consider how to do it, I feel a pat on my shoulder. When I turn, Uncle Luke is there, beaming at me. "Nice to see you again, Jonny boy."

I'm not going to make a scene. I'm going to hold my shit together for Pete. For Sidney. I shake him off. "Go stand somewhere else."

Uncle Luke flinches in his new Armani suit and Mezlan wingtips. "That's hardly an appropriate greeting for your favorite uncle." His light hair is slicked back, out of his eyes. His skin is tanned like he's been spending all his free time on his yacht.

I can't stand it. I'm going crazy worrying about Cass, and I can't help it. I blame the motherfucker. If Luke hadn't made me turn on Cassie, she wouldn't have met and married Mark. I could have saved her from a lifetime of pain if this prick hadn't interfered. I round on him and shove him hard into the marble column. "You're not my favorite anything, anymore. You're a putrid piece of shit too low to acknowledge, but since I'm here with my hands around your neck, I'll elaborate. You screwed with the wrong man, you fuckfaced pisshole of a human being."

Luke laughs lightly so I shove him harder. I feel eyes on me, Sean's. Right now no one else sees. They're looking at the bird, watching Sidney and mom fight over the perch placement.

Luke's hands wrap around mine and try to rip them away, but I don't back down. "You nearly killed her, and for what? So you could win some pissing match with Mom?" I shake my head and drop my hands. "You're not worth it."

Luke stands there stunned. "Jon, I never—"

"Don't." It's a one-word warning with more venom than I thought I had in me.

Sean's behind me a moment later. His voice is even, careful. "Why don't you go check on Cassie?" I turn and glance at him, wondering if he knows where she is. He couldn't. Sean's expression is unreadable, as always, but there's a twinge of compassion in his tone. I can't miss it.

"Mom and Sidney will be debating where that bird stands for the next hour and then it's food after that. Your mind is elsewhere, and there's clearly an issue between you and Luke."

I glare at Sean, torn. I want to spill my guts and tell him everything. I know he'd help me if I asked, but I'm too fucking proud to say it. I shake my head. "There's nothing here worth worrying about. What's done is done. Keep this asshole away from me and there's nothing to worry about."

Uncle Luke laughs nervously. "Jon, give me a chance to explain."

I can't handle it. His arrogance, the way he completely disregards what he did to Cassie, to me. I'm in his face hissing, "There's nothing you could say to fix the damage you've done. There's no fucking way to undo a goddamned drop of the misery you've caused. Stay the fuck away from me or you won't like what happens."

Uncle Luke is still a Ferro, although a borderline crazy one. His lips snake into a smile that reminds me of mom. "I could end you, boy. You've been a thorn in this family's side for far too long."

"I'd like to see you try—"

Before the exchange continues, Sean steps between us, grabs my arm. He snaps at Luke, "Enough, Uncle Luke. You, of all people, should know better than to threaten your own. You," Sean jerks my arm, but I yank it away, "come with me. Now."

I follow him up the side of the nave and shove through the side door onto the city street outside. The sounds of horns and engines rumbling fill my ears as Sean rushes down the steps and abruptly turns to look up at me. I step down slowly, one at a time, my hands deep in my pockets.

His voice is clipped, features irritated. "You've been disowned, Jon. You know that means if something happens to Mom, everything goes to Luke. That man wants everyone to think he's a moron, but he's not. The bastard has a long memory and doesn't forgive shit."

I lean on the railing and stand a foot above him on the last step. "Tell me something I don't know."

"He could erase you, make it look like you were never here. I've been keeping my eye on him. Why do you think Mom banished him in the first place? It wasn't because he was nuts. It's because she needed him contained. Bribery only goes so far. Luke knows everything is his once Mom is out of the way. I don't want that, and neither do you."

"I don't give a fuck what Luke does."

Sean tenses, his jaw tightening, and he steps up to me until we're nose to nose. "Yes you do. That fucker will cleanse the line and eradicate any threats, which includes you. I know what he did to you, to Cassie. I get it. But this isn't the time for a pissing match. You'll lose."

"Then what do I do?" I'm angry, pissed I was so fucking stupid. I didn't see it before, but what Sean's saying lines up. Luke was never harmless.

"We wait. We bide our time until the most opportune moment and then take all of it, push Luke out, and make sure he doesn't come back. He hit you where it hurts once already. He won't hold back a second time. He sees you now, they all do."

I shake my head and laugh, "I don't know what you're talking about."

"Cut the shit, Jonny. They know you're smarter than you let on, and they know you've got way more than a hard-on for that girl." Sean glances down the street and then back at me. He walks up the steps, heading back inside. Before he pulls open the door, he says, "Play nice and when the time is right, Pete and I will help you take him down—together. In the meantime, keep Cassie close." His eyes rest on mine, saying a million other things that'll never pass over his lips. There are whispers of loyalty, understanding, and protection. It's what I've wanted from Sean from the beginning, a promise of something I thought vanished long ago. Now it's back, staring me in the face. I could spit in his face, write him off like everyone else, but I don't.

Sean's my brother. I've got his back, and he has mine. I nod once, curtly and smile in a way that infuriates him. It's cocky, arrogant, and charming all at once. "It's good to have you back."

Sean watches me for a moment, barely breathing. He tips his head, a slight smile playing at the corners of his lips, then disappears into the church without another word.

*****

I speed all the way back to Cassie's apartment, rushing down the stairs and through the door. I'm huffing. She's sitting on the couch with a cup of frozen yogurt in her hands. Beth is sitting next to her, and they're both smiling.

"Cassie." I practically skid to a stop and for a second everything is fine. There's a smile on her face. I was afraid I'd find her in her bedroom crying. Not going to the doctor with her killed me, but I had to keep reminding myself that this isn't my battle. It's hers. And I'll be there for backup when she needs me, but today wasn't that day.

"Jon." She looks up at me with those warm brown eyes. She hands Beth her yogurt and stands up. "How about a walk?"

"Nice tux, 007." Beth teases. "Anything happen at the rehearsal for the wedding of the century?"

"Nope. Unless you count the vulture being batshit crazy, but we already knew that." I tug off my tux jacket. It's not a good outfit to walk around in.

But Cassie puts a hand on my shoulder and stops me. "It looks nice. You look dashing. Leave it on for a bit?"

I nod and follow her outside. The night air is humid. My hair sticks to my forehead. I'm a sweaty mess. I was so worried about her. The rehearsal took much longer than anticipated, then the shit with Luke and Sean. I thought I'd be home hours ago. I'm glad she's smiling, but I'm still worried. "So, was Dr. Bellamy a heinous bitch or what?"

She laughs lightly and slips her small hand into mine. "No, she was very kind."

"I thought you might like her."

"She cares about you a lot."

I nod once and glance over at her. "Bellamy seems to sense when someone is hurting, and she sincerely cares about her patients. It's refreshing. She'll do anything to help. I've seen her make house calls, Cassie, and charge nothing. It's a crusade for her, a way to undo some of the evil in the world."

"I can tell." She's looking at the asphalt, as we head down the street.

The douche across from us is watching. He's always watching, which makes me nervous. There could be some bad shit going on over there—Cassie and Beth are way too close to it.

"Well, what'd she say?" I hate prying like this. Asking her that bluntly feels like a dick thing to do, but I need to know if she's okay. I need to know if there's hope.

Cassie's lips curve up, and she looks over at me. We're at the corner now, and she's stopped. Facing me, she holds my hand and traces a pattern on the back of it while she talks. "She said you told her to tell me anything I wanted to know about you. You didn't have to do that."

"I know, but if there was anything that could help you, I wanted her to use it."

"It was sweet, and kind, and perfect. Like you." Her voice is fragile, with a slight quiver in it. I lean down and kiss the top of her head, holding her tight for a moment.

"I love you, Cass."

"I love you, too, Jon." She steps back and smiles up at me. "She said there are ways to make it better. Last night, the main thing that upset me was that scar. It made me feel sick, and it hurt. She said that was something that didn't have to happen, and she told me how to work on it." Cassie holds up a finger and smirks. "It's very dirty therapy, and it's the kind of thing I don't have to do alone. Actually, she said it might help me with other variables if we both did it."

"So, you're going to be all right? She can help you?"

Cassie grins at the ground and nods. "Yes. I have an appointment again next week. She's going to show me some things. In the meantime, I have books to read. It helps explain what happened, and why my body is stuck like this. It'll take a while, but eventually, we can be together, and I won't feel like puking on you. I might even like it!" Her face flames red and she pulls away. "God, that sounds awful."

I grab her arm and pull her into my chest. "It sounds wonderful." I sigh contentedly and try to stop smiling. I hold her like that, her small body wrapped in my arms, her head tucked beneath my chin and feel emotions slip over me like a warm blanket on a cold day.

She's going to be all right.

She didn't shut me out.

She still wants me.

It's a fucking miracle.

As I smile like a kid on the corner, a low rumble shakes the street beneath our feet. I lift my head, but before I can say anything, it becomes a roar. Fire explodes through the windows of the drug den down the block swallowing the house whole.

Kam stands on the curb, leaning against his car. His hands are in the pockets of his black pants seemingly unaffected by the wave of heat and flames. Beneath his battered brown leather jacket, a white t-shirt clings to his dark skin. The fucker torched that building and stayed to watch it burn.

After the roar quiets, Kam turns and looks at us. His expression is hard when he glances at me, but when his gaze shifts to Cassie, a light smile pulls at his mouth. Shit.

Cassie gasps and looks up at me. "He did that on purpose."

"Yeah, he did."

"And we saw it."

"No, we didn't see anything." This is trouble I don't want, not for her or me. "I'll make sure he knows it. Go inside, and get Beth. We're getting the fuck out of here and never coming back. Go, now." I push her back, and as she races toward the apartment, I walk toward Kam.

The man doesn't move much. He finally glances at me when I step in front of him. The warmth from the burning house is torching my back. I wouldn't stand here, but when I glance over my shoulder, I know why he does. He has a good line of sight. If anyone gets out, he'll see it. And put a bullet in their head.

I stand with my feet a shoulder's width apart and copy his stance. Slipping my hands into my pockets, I say, "Nice day for a fire."

The flames dance in Kam's eyes. He doesn't look at me. His gaze is locked on that house. "Amongst other things, I suppose so."

"My back was turned. What happened?"

Kam turns his head and looks at me. This is going to turn into some complicated shit. "You saw the explosion, Ferro. Don't pretend you didn't. I don't give a fuck about you, but you don't need to worry. Nothing will happen to your girl. I like her."

"I can see that." I sound like a prick, but guys like this take what they want, and no one is ever fucking with Cassie again. Not while I'm alive.

"You don't see shit." He pushes off the car and turns toward me, draping an arm over my shoulder. I know he has a gun, and I don't. This is going to get real ugly, real fast. "The thing is, that girl had a hard life. I see it on her face. I don't like people who treat women like bitches. They're not. How are you treating her, Ferro? From what I know of you, I haven't a fucking clue why you've been there so often. Why not take her to your apartment in the city, fuck her brains out in style, and then dump her like you always do?"

I react. I shove my elbow into his chest, and his arm drops. I round on him, grabbing his shirt collar and squeezing hard. "You don't know what you're talking about, Kam. If you do anything to hurt her, I'll—"

The fucker starts laughing at me. There's a cold barrel pressing into my stomach. I release him, but I don't step back. "Again, you misunderstood me, friend." He spits out the last word sharply. "I suggest you figure out who your allies are quickly because you seem confused."

He presses the barrel harder then pulls it away.

"An ally? You?"

He nods once then turns his attention back to the house. The cops and fire trucks won't show up until it's nearly burned to the ground. They stopped coming down these streets a long time ago. Too many lives lost in the call of duty. Now they shrink back and let the drug dealers kill each other. Then, they come clean up the mess after it's over.

Kam flicks an ash off his coat and stares straight ahead. "I took care of a problem for you, for Cassie, actually. There was a dipshit in a red truck waiting by the old lady's house a few nights back. He asked if Cassie lived there and I said yes, invited him in. The asshole proceeded to tell me that she's his bitch, married. The woman ran off and is having fun fucking some rich guy. He didn't seem to realize who you are."

Shit. Kam didn't do what I think he did. There's no way. But he did. I understand before he says the rest. As I watch the flames lick the eaves of the house, gasping for breath through the blown windows, the fire takes on a whole new light.

Kam is utterly calm, his face placid as he continues. "I have issues with men who treat women that way. My shrink says it's a deep insecurity from watching some prick batter my sisters, but I think it was watching my mother get backhanded with a shovel that put me over the top. I killed that motherfucker without a second of doubt, and since then, when I see their kind—the ones who think they can get away with it—I make sure they don't get away with shit. Call it justice for assholes." His gaze cuts to the side.

"How long has he been watching her?"

"From what I gather, you kicked his ass, and he found Cassie's place the next day. He had plans for you, friend. The dumb shit told me what he was going to do to you and then to Cassie. Arrogant fuck." Anger rolls off him for a moment, but he reins it in, a cool, emotionless expression sliding back across his face.

"Why the fire?"

Kam smirks. "He deserved to burn in Hell, and since I can't be sure there's an afterlife, I made sure he got his before he checked out. Tell Cassie she doesn't have to worry about him anymore. Use discretion with the details. She won't like this."

No shit. Vengeance isn't her thing. "I hear you."

Kam stands there a moment longer before turning to me. "The story that'll be in the papers tomorrow is that this drug transaction went south with the dealers inside. The meth lab in the basement is a highly volatile thing. Just another day on this side of the tracks."

Cassie comes rushing out with Beth in tow. Beth starts shoving their stuff into the car as Cassie rushes over to us. She looks up at Kam, unafraid. "Are you all right? You're burned, Kam." She reaches for a spot on his temple, but he doesn't let her touch it.

He catches her hand in his and smiles at her. "I'm fine, Cassie. You should get out of here for a few days unless you like talking to cops."

She nods and he drops her hand.

Kam glances at me, the warmth for Cassie still in his eyes, and leans in. He speaks in a hushed tone so that Cassie can't hear. "You owe me a favor, Ferro." He holds out his hand, and I take it, shaking it firmly.

"Agreed," I reply in his ear.

When I pull away, he nods once and talks to Cass for a moment.

I'm glad someone else was helping watch out for her. I should be horrified that her husband is in there, being burned alive, but I'm not. That fucker was so determined to hurt her nothing short of death would have stopped him. He got too close too many times. I'd been considering how to remove him from the equation and not liking my options. Cassie would never forgive me if I'd done this. I owe Kam a huge debt, one that I'll be happy to pay.

I pull the car away from the apartment, Cassie by my side and Beth shoved in the backseat. I drive away, watching the flames in the rearview mirror. Today is a turning point for Cassie, for us. The past is burning behind us, and I'm glad.

CHAPTER 28
CASSIE

The new noises—the constant traffic and blaring car horns—take some getting used to, but our height goes a long way to muffle the sounds on the street. We're in the penthouse with a stellar view of Central Park. The windows wrap around Jon's apartment, creating a panoramic frame for the city skyline.

I'm perched on Jon's sofa, wearing his robe, a cup of coffee in my hands while I watch the sunrise. Beth is still asleep in the guest bedroom. On the coffee table, an old newspaper lays open to a brief article about a meth lab explosion. I continually worried about Mark showing up, hurting me, and dragging me back with him. But that's over now. He got so close to me it makes me shiver to consider the possibilities.

Mark was watching us from across the street, waiting for the opportune time to strike, but completely unaware of the drug deal going wrong in the basement below him. When the meth lab blew, it killed everyone inside the house—including Mark. The authorities assumed he was just another drug dealer, but I know better. I know why he was there in that specific building. He was there to watch me.

I don't have to worry about Mark ever again. I don't have to see him at a divorce hearing. I don't have to get a restraining order or press charges when he comes after me again. After all those years of running and hiding, it's over. I'm free from him. I no longer need to jump at every sound, wondering if it's him.

My legs are curled up under me. Since we abandoned the apartment Beth and I shared, I've spent a blissful series of nights next to Jon in his huge bed. Last night he held me for a long time, kissing me lightly as we spooned. For the first time in a long time, I feel safe. Content.

Beth staggers out moaning something that sounds like troll-speak for coffee and plops down next to me. She takes my cup and chugs it. When she finishes, she turns her head slowly and glances at me. "You skipped work again last night. Cheater."

I grin. "Jon said he wanted me to wait until it was done to see all the changes he made."

Her brows lift up into her bangs, and she bobs her head up and down. "That's the truth. So, do you want me to tell you what's going on?"

"Don't ruin his surprise!" I smack her with one of the small white throw pillows. "He's been working so hard on it, and he seems really excited." I have no clue what he did, but he's proud, so I want to hear about it. It's hard not to take her bait.

Beth takes the pillow and sinks back into the couch. Her arm flops to the side as she rolls to set the mug down on the coffee table before hugging the assaulting pillow to her chest. "Fine, but your boy did a good thing. I love my job."

"Wow, I never thought I'd hear you say that."

"I know, right? It's really something. Even Bruce is speechless." After a moment, she tickles me with her bare foot. "How are you doing? I'd be an emotional train wreck if I were you. You okay?"

She's referring to Mark. I nod and settle back into the fluffy pillows to watch shades of amber and coral streak across the city skyline. Shadows shift against the ground below, but I'm up in the clouds watching the early morning sunlight spill across the sky and pierce the space between the steel towers that make up this amazing city.

"I'm doing better than I thought. He's dead, Beth. Gone. I don't have to jump every time I hear a noise. He'll never be in my life again. You have no idea how good that feels. It's like that entire mistake never happened. Well, for the most part."

Beth knows what I'm talking about. It's a sensitive topic, but I found that talking to someone helps. She has ideas that Jon doesn't think of, mainly because she's a woman, and she understands some things differently because of it. "Have you been able to be with him?"

"A little." My face flames when I think about it.

Beth notices. "That's more than a little. Seriously? You were able to, and you're ok?"

I'm bright red, but I'm happy. I nod and avoid her eyes. "The cream they compounded for me worked really well." The doctor suggested it after seeing me. It has a topical analgesic in it to minimize the pain and oversensitivity of the scar.

"Yeah?"

I take a sip of coffee and then nod. "Yeah, it helped a lot. I thought I wouldn't be able to feel anything, but it didn't do that. It just numbed the scar. Jon was gentle, and it worked. I didn't cry. It didn't make me feel sick. It felt really good to be that close to him, to be with him. I didn't think I'd ever be able to, you know?"

Beth is lying on her side, watching the sun come up. "I know, and I'm so happy for you. When things down there don't work right, it sucks. It's manageable, but I'm glad you don't have your shop totally closed for business if you know what I mean."

"Everyone knows what you mean." I look at her and giggle.

She's right about that. I could have lived without having sex again, but I'm glad I didn't have to. I'd rather start over, figure it all out, and do it this way. The fact that Jon is so patient and tender astounds me. He knows the savage side of sex, the carnal kisses and hot bodies twisted together, but this kind of lovemaking is new to him, too.

It's not hard and sharp with sweat and screams. It's gentle and adoring, tender and evocative. He brings me high and undoes me. As I come back down, I lie in his arms and feel his breath on my cheek.

I delight in the little things overlooked by most people. The way his hands hold my hips, the curve of his back as he pushes into me, the soft whispers of his voice as he asks me if I like what he's doing. I've never been so open with another person, so vulnerable and elated to be that way. I don't feel caged with him, and we're not missing out on anything. We've both had rough sex, been used, and burned. Monica messed him up badly. If she hadn't come and gone, I don't know who he would have been, but I think meeting me later after all this happened brought him back.

Sex isn't a game. It's not something to take. It's something to give, something to share. There's a gentle dance, a back and forth of emotion that fills my body and makes me shatter in his arms.

I didn't know it could be like this, and I worried that Jon wanted the other—the rough possession. But he doesn't. Those days have passed for him. This path is terrifying because it requires all of him. It's not just his body. It's his mind and every emotion, too. No one lives like that intentionally, even for a moment, because it feels like he can crush me so easily. There are no walls up, nothing to protect me if he changes his mind. It requires a massive amount of trust for both of us. It's not easy to do, even if only for a little bit at a time. People don't talk this way. They aren't so forthcoming, but when we are—

when we finally let our walls drop—we can truly become one.

Beth sits up and rubs her eyes. "So, what's the plan for the day? I heard Jon was taking you to the helipad later."

Smiling, I nod and set my mug down on the table. "Yeah, he said he wanted to show me something after I check out the new Club Ferro."

"Cool, do you know where you're going?" A grin spills across her face, and she beams at me. "Because I do! It's so awesome!" She clasps her hands giddy.

My jaw drops. "How'd you find out?"

"I heard him talking to someone about it."

"Tell me. No, wait. Don't." I make a face, push out my lower lip and bite my cheek. "Yeah, tell me."

Beth laughs and shakes her head. "No way. But I will give you a tip—wear that sundress he bought you. You look pretty in it, and it's comfy."

Only twelve hours until tonight. I can't wait that long.

CHAPTER 29
CASSIE

We speed out to Long Island, to the club. Jon is driving with an excited vibe about him. He's wearing a nice suit and has a light dusting of stubble on his jaw. His eyes look brighter when he doesn't shave. That dark hair makes the blue so rich and vibrant.

He has that chunky watch on his wrist that cost a fortune and a pair of black pants that hug his ass in a way that's hard not to notice. It's like staring at the sun. I think angels sing while he walks, and it takes everything I have within me to not pinch him right then.

He's got a soft button-down shirt on with no tie, and his jacket is across the shallow backseat. He downshifts, making the car purr, and cuts through traffic.

I adjust the strap on my sundress and look over at him. "So, are you going to tell me anything about our dinner plans?"

"Nope." Jon grins, shifts again, and bobs around another car.

"Not even a hint?"

He glances over at me, his hand on the gearshift, and sighs. "Okay, a little one. We're not having dinner at the club."

My face crunches up. Unless he means crackers and peanuts, I wouldn't have said the club serves dinner at all. His meaning finally dawns on me. "Wow, you serve food now?"

"Wait and see." After a few more turns, we're pulling into a newly paved parking lot.

It looks like a different building. Club Ferro glows in purple neon on the outside of a limestone building with thick dark wood beams surrounding the front door and supporting the roof. Glowing in the dim light, the building resembles a little French chateau lost in New York.

"Jon, it's beautiful." I don't know how he got this done so fast. It's only been a few weeks since he bought it, but it's barely recognizable.

After we park, he circles the car to open my door and takes my hand. When I step out, I notice the custom brickwork on the path to the brand new front door. It's not even in the same spot in the wall. Instead, we're standing in front of two double doors facing the street. The dark new color and intricate wrought iron scrolling contrast nicely against the pale stone veneer. It's beautiful. It makes me wonder what I'm going to find inside.

He pulls the door open, and we enter the main room. The floors have been ripped up and replaced with dark, polished concrete. The walls are dark brown leather attached with decorative golden brads. The rich purple chairs are still here, but now they look like they belong. The light fixtures cast the perfect amount of golden light on the tables. The biggest change, however, is the stage area. Instead of three platforms, there's one large stage minus the poles. A massive velvet curtain hangs closed across the front of it. A spotlight shines down on the heavy plum colored drapery, illuminating the ruched fabric and golden tassels.

I blink rapidly and look around. The girls are wearing dark purple corsets with fitted jackets and short black skirts. They all have matching thick black velvet headbands and tight chignons at the napes of their necks.

Gretchen sees us and rushes over. "Sorry, I didn't mean to run, but this is more than I ever dreamed. Jon, you took my ideas and made them even better. This, just, OMG!" She covers her mouth with her hand and blinks rapidly. "Thank you! It's a marvelous place to be, and I'm beyond excited I get to work here." She squeals and rushes off.

I glance at Jon. "You planned this with Gretchen?"

"She has an interior design degree she wasn't using. I saw it in her file when I bought the place. I brainstormed with her and a few other girls who had hidden talents, and we came up with this. It's not a strip club anymore, but that revenue was too important to the top dancers to take away. So we talked about it and came up with this idea. It's a vintage-style burlesque and dinner club for men."

I blink at him. "Is that code for a fancy strip club?"

He shakes his head, holds out a hand and leads me to a booth. We slide in, and he hands me a leather bound menu. "No, it's not. The stage is for performances. They'll start one in a moment. Instead of exposing everything, it's more of a traditional burlesque—it's about the dance. The girls are never completely naked. That's not the point. It's about movement, empowerment, and the woman showing the men what she thinks is a powerful display of seduction. To choreograph our new shows, I hired a woman who trained as a classical ballet dancer. She fell in love with Betty Paige style pinups and started a neo-burlesque revival a few years back in England."

I don't understand. "So the other girls got demoted to waitresses?"

"No, they're all part of the show. It's a full-blown production. Tonight is a practice run, a dress rehearsal if you will. The club doesn't officially reopen until next week. We rebranded, and advertisements are running. My hope is to pull in a more refined crowd with more money. The girls can work less, and it'll keep this place from turning into a money pit. It's possible we could even turn a profit in the first year— which is unusual."

I'm about to tell him how proud I am that he did this. He pulled on the talents hidden in plain sight and turned this place into something unique. Before I can say anything, people pour out of the wing of the stage and sit down in a small area. Their brass instruments flash in their hands as they take their seats and quickly ready themselves. The horns play a quick jazz number then the curtain pulls up toward the ceiling and then back to the side.

Jon sits back and folds his arms across his chest. I feel his gaze shift and look away fast, as if he wants to know what I think.

White smoke fills the stage, flooding it from somewhere in the darkness behind. As the music pulses through me, several former dancers appear in black corsets and lavish headdresses adorned with feathers and sparkles. They're pulling out a carved wooden horse, the kind that belongs on a carousel. There's a woman in a pink gown sitting on the saddle. She jumps off and steps in beat to the music, dancing with a huge smile on her face.

Her pink skirt brushes the floor as she spins. She moves gracefully, taking elegant steps across the stage. The other girls join her. It's more of a musical production at this point than a strip tease.

The woman in the center wears a sparkling pink corset with a sheer skirt that swishes at her ankles. Her headdress has tall plumes of pink and white feathers adorned with sparkling jewels. She has bracelets on her wrists and silver shoes with towering heels, but they're not stripper shoes. She can walk and dance easily, even with the tall heel.

She suddenly turns away, and her sheer skirt drops on the offbeat. It flutters to the floor as she spins back toward us with a smile. Her wrists are above her head as she dances. Her hips shimmy in something resembling a belly dance then things speed up.

As she spins again, her corset comes off. Underneath, she wears pasties on her nipples and a bra that looks like jewelry with little bits of silver dangling between crystals. Combined with the pasties, it looks pretty. The women dancing next to her don't remove anything. They're dancing with the woman in pink, forming a kick line, then move her back to the carousel horse.

While one woman dances in front, the two in back help lift the main dancer up. She sits sidesaddle, leans backward then uses those long, shapely legs to make the horse rock. Her jewels shimmer in the bright light as she rocks, thrusting her front leg up with each downbeat of the music.

As the melody crescendos, she kicks once, twice, and a third time, then as they hold the final note, she holds her leg in the air. Golden fireworks sparkle in front of the horse and spray into the air, backlighting the dancers with a warm, glittering glow. They all end in unison, and the stage curtain drops with an abrupt swish, shielding them from the audience's view.

My jaw hits the table, and I turn to Jon. "Oh. My. God!"

Jon looks nervous. His brow is pinched, and he leans forward in the booth. His slouching arrogant attitude vanishes for the moment. "Is that a good ohmigod or a bad ohmigod? Last night I could tell, but right now—not so much."

I blurt out a loud laugh and swat at his shoulder. "Jon!"

He grabs my hands and talks so fast I can't get a word in edgewise. "There's nothing on the island like this. It was a risk, bringing her here and turning this place into a club. I wanted to turn it into something you'd be proud of, something different. I wanted to offer people a Vegas-style show right in their own backyard. Talk to me, Cass. Was it that bad? Was it—"

I lean in and kiss him to make him stop talking. The tension flows out of his shoulders, and he melts the moment our lips touch. When I pull back, I say, "I loved it. I didn't know what to expect at first, but the combination of the music, chorus dancers, and the main dancer—Oh, Jon, it's amazing!"

"Really?"

"Yes! Really! That was less than two minutes on stage, and I'm grinning like an idiot, dying to see more. I think you nailed it. A place like this will do fantastic here. So, you've kept the bar, added food and hired more waitresses?"

I glance around. There are way more employees here than usual. Jon nods and watches me, his beautiful face smiling.

"Yeah, and during the final number, well—I think it's better if I show you."

He cues the band to start playing again. The curtains rise quickly, and the main dancer is now wearing a fluffy red dress and performing a different dance. It's fast, flashy, and fun. By the end, she's wearing a G-string, a crystal bra that somehow still covers her nipples, golden heels and outlandish red feathers above her head. Every inch of her moves powerfully, confidently.

I don't notice the waitresses moving around, but they get close to the stage, grab a circular tray and spin. On stage, the main dancer spins high in the air, lifted by two of the girls, while the rest spin around, suddenly wearing less clothing. I can't tell where the corsets went, but all the girls don short flouncy skirts barely covering their cheeks with shimmering black bras. They hold their trays in front and dance in unison. As the band reprises the song, golden sparks shoot from the sides of the trays and shower down from the ceiling.

I'm gasping, clutching the edge of the table. I glance at Jon and back at the women who are holding one arm in the air awaiting further instructions. "You need to let women come in here. Don't make it a men's only club."

Jon seems surprised. "What? Why?"

"Because that was the coolest thing I've ever seen! You shouldn't cut out half the population. Women will want to see it, too. It's amazing."

The dancers are still standing there, arms up. Jon stands and claps. "Well, that was our first show, and it went really well. Congratulations, ladies!"

As everyone starts clapping, a million questions pop up in my head. Why don't the sparks burn the floor dancers? How do the feathers stay on their heads while they're moving around like that? Where did she get that crystal bra? It's awesome! I want one. But mainly I want to learn how to dance like that!

Bruce walks over as Jon goes to take care of some things. "Hello, Cassie."

I smile up at him. "Bruce! What are you doing now?"

"Same thing as before for the most part, security. Making sure no one goes backstage, tossing out troublemakers and that kind of stuff."

I stare at the stage and watch Jon standing there, all his weight on one leg, with that perfect ass looking yummy in those pants.

"So, what other changes are in the works?"

Bruce has his beefy arms folded across his chest. "Possible daylight hours and classes."

"Classes for what?"

"Cooking. The kitchen is huge. Ferro put in multiple stations. He said something about classes for man meals and dancing."

"Dancing?"

Bruce points toward the stage. "Yeah, you can come in and learn how to do that."

My eyes go wide, and I try not to fangirl squeal. I don't know where to put my hands. They go to my face, and I slap my cheeks as I grin wildly. "No. Way. Don't even toy with me, Bruce! Is that for real?"

An amused look spreads across his normally impassive face. "That's what the boss said. Open for dinner and shows at night, cooking and classes during the day."

I can't help it. I love it even more, now. A giddy giggle works its way up inside of me, and I scoot out of the booth and rush toward Jon.

I crash into him from behind, laughing. "The classes? Are they real? Is it a thing?"

Jon stops talking to the bandleader and turns to face me. He pries me off his waist and holds both my hands. Looking down at me, he asks, "Do you really like it?"

"I love it. You took the best things people had to offer, made it fun, and then added a how-to-be-awesome section. Jon,"

I stroke a finger over his temple, "you have this creative mastermind living in here. You need to let him out more often, because OMG!" I gush, doubling over at the waist as I say it. "This is amazing! You're amazing!"

Before he can reply, someone behind me says, "I'm inclined to agree."

I turn quickly and see Sean standing behind us, his hands clasped in front of him. He's wearing a black sweater that clings to his chest and a pair of strategically tattered jeans. He's holding a helmet in his hands and studying the changed surroundings.

Jon stiffens. "How long have you been here?"

"Long enough."

"Sean, I don't need any shit from you right now."

"That wasn't my intention before and isn't my intention now. I meant what I said the last time we spoke." His voice is flat, but something in his eyes makes me know he's sincere, though I have no idea what they last said to each other. Jon didn't say anything to me about it.

"Sean, I don't know what I want anymore. I'm sick of trying to meet other people's expectations and failing."

"So go your own way. Make your own mistakes. Life's too short to live it for someone else." Sean shifts his weight and sets his helmet down on a table.

Jon stares at him in disbelief. "Why are you here, Sean?"

Sean bows his head and glances to the side, his gaze landing on me. "To tell you what I should have said the other day— that no matter what happens with Uncle Luke or anyone else, I'm here. I'm not leaving again. I'm here for Pete and you. Anything you need, Jon. I mean it. I moved back into my place in the city. I'm home for good."

Jon hesitates, shaking his head. I think he's going to give his brother a verbal lashing, but, instead, Jon lifts his arms and wraps them around Sean. He slaps his back twice, and Sean does the same. They say something to each other, something I can't hear before pulling back.

Then Sean turns toward the door with his helmet tucked under his arm. Just before he crosses the threshold, he pauses, turns, and says, "Don't let that one get away. She's good for you. She sees you, Jonny." He doesn't wait for a reply. Sean's gone.

CHAPTER 30
CASSIE

I chatter about the club and ask him what else he has planned on the way to the heliport. At least, I think that's where we're going until he passes it. I arch a brow at him. "Where are we going?"

"You'll see."

I glance out the window, watching the city streets fly by. It's late, and there's no traffic. We dip south of the city and enter

New Jersey. Jon winds around a few streets in an industrial area. "Did you bring me out here to whack me and throw my body in one of these storage yards?"

Jon snorts and glances over at me. "Do you normally worry about that when you're out with me?'

"Not in a while. But at first? Yeah. Why did you think I wouldn't go out with you?"

"Because you thought I was a sex god and couldn't control yourself?"

I double over in my seat laughing. "Oh, please! It's because I thought you'd get us both eaten by gators. I heard how you liked to tempt them by walking along the spillway." The seatbelt engages and locks. I tug at the strap, but it only presses me closer against the seat until I'm too stuck to move.

Jon stifles a laugh. "So, how's it going?"

I'm pressing the button to release the strap, but it won't click. There's too much pressure on it. "I'm stuck." I drop my arms and slouch against the restraints. "Breathing's going to be an issue."

"Calm down. We're here." He pulls into a narrow driveway, passing a sign that says Teterboro Airport.

Jon pulls over for a second and unbuckles me. "I just need to drive past the gate. You good?"

I nod sheepishly. Jon leans in and presses a kiss to my lips. "Good."

He pulls up to the gate, gives the tail number of the plane for security reasons, and they let us pass through. Curiosity is killing me. This is the airport for the freakishly rich, not the helipad. "Jon, where are we going?"

Jon parks the car next to a huge plane. He glances over at me while he turns off the engine. "Somewhere you want to see."

I still have no clue. Disney World? I'm going to ride on Small World until I puke! I squee inwardly, but act badass on the outside. "Okay. We're walking there, right?"

He smiles. "Get out of the car, wiseass."

I giggle as we walk up to the plane. Standing this close to an airliner is impressive. They look big from the window, but I never realized the tires are taller than me. The rest of it is like a flying building. It's insane, and we're going to be the only ones on it.

Jon talks to the captain as I head up the stairs.

Confused, I ask, "You're not flying?"

Jon shakes his head. "Not tonight. Go pick out a spot for us to sit."

I smile at him before I reach the top landing and pass through the door. After saying hello to the other co-pilot, I turn through another doorway and stare. It's a living room complete with white leather couches, chairs, a dining table, and even a chandelier. The back wall is mirrored, making the space look twice as large. I walk back and flop into a chair.

"Holy shit," I say, running my fingers appreciatively over the leather. It's supple, like those chairs in the tux store. I know Jon has money in theory, but I never remember in practice. When I met him, he was always in a trailer with me, and, more recently, he's been sleeping on my floor. His New York City apartment is worth more than I can imagine, but this? This plane is a luxury that puts his wealth in perspective.

Jonathan Ferro is a billionaire.

I feel a hand on my shoulder and jump. "Sorry, Cassie. I said something, but you didn't hear me."

I touch his hand and look up at him. His jacket drapes over his arm, and his hair is perfectly messy. Bright blue eyes sparkle with excitement.

"This is, wow!"

A crooked smile tugs at the corner of his mouth. "You're always shocked by my wealth."

I nod in slow motion. "Because it's more than I can imagine. If I had a little money, I'd buy a Hyundai and pay off my credit cards. If I won the lottery, I'd buy a souped-up Genesis and maybe get some new clothes."

"Wait. If you won the lottery you'd get a nicer Hyundai? On purpose?"

I nod. "It's a pretty car."

He smiles and sits in the chair opposite me. "It is." He doesn't tease me even though my dreams are cheap. I'd be the only rich girl clipping coupons and double-checking that my jeans are on sale even if my bank account was stuffed to the gills.

"This life is so far beyond me..." I shake my head. "You're this great man, you have so much, and yet—it's not who you are."

He arches a dark brow. "You sound surprised."

"I am. I thought if someone had all this stuff there'd be no way he'd slum it with a stripper and sleep on the basement floor. Sure there's carpet, but it's cheap and old. It feels like sleeping on cement. You could have been here."

"I didn't want to be here. I wanted you. I still do."

I feel small and nervous. I avoid looking at him as I try to make sense of this. I'm not jealous, or mad. I don't know what I am. I guess it just shows how different we are, and that scares me.

Then he's there, in front of me. Jon takes my hands and crouches in front of me. "Cassie, I love you. If you want to fly commercial, I don't mind. We can wait in line at JFK airport and take off three or four hours from now. I don't care as long as I'm with you."

I feel silly and shake my head. "No, that's okay. I like this. It's just a lot to comprehend."

He reaches for the seatbelt and buckles me in. "There, now you can't get away."

We both laugh as the captain announces we're ready to take off.

CHAPTER 31
CASSIE

Once we're in the air, Jon unfolds a tablecloth and sets the table. He grabs food from the storage area at the front of the plane and tells me I can wash up in the back if I'd like. I rise and walk to the glass door. When I pull it open, I freeze in stunned shock. There's another room, as large as this one, with a big bed on one side and a long couch on the other.

I call back to Jon over my shoulder. "There's a bedroom in here."

He laughs, stops what he's doing and looks up at me. "I know, I thought you'd want a place to sleep. This is an international flight."

I turn on my heel, shocked. "What?"

He walks toward me with a coy smile on that beautiful face, hands behind his back. "I'm taking you to Paris. We're going to walk hand in hand along the Seine. I'm going to take you to my favorite café for lunch and spoil you until you beg me to stop."

The corners of my mouth rise and fall repeatedly as I try not to overreact. "I don't have my passport."

"I have it."

"How'd you find it?"

"Beth helped me. I didn't feel comfortable digging through your things looking for it. She had no such qualms once she found out what I was planning."

"Are you serious? We're going to Paris? THE Paris? In France?" Jon nods, grinning, and I rush into his arms, squeezing him tight. "I always wanted to go there. I thought I'd never have the chance."

Jon holds me tight and says into my ear, "I thought I'd never get the chance to tell you I love you. I thought I'd never get the chance to taste your lips, and I thought any kiss I got from you would be stolen."

He pulls away to look down at me, then leans in to press his mouth to mine. "You have no idea how many times I fantasized about doing that. Now, I'm going to serve you an amazing dinner," he spins me around toward the bedroom and points over my shoulder, "then we are going in there for dessert. I'm going to spoil you in any way you want, all you have to do is ask." He wraps his arms around my shoulders and whispers in my ear. "In the morning, we'll wake up, shower, and take a walk along the Seine."

I love the feel of his arms around me and the sound of his voice. My hands come up and hold onto his. I'm so happy I can barely speak.

"This is extraordinary," I whisper.

He kisses my temple lightly. "You're extraordinary."

He presses another kiss to the side of my cheek. "Beautiful."

Then another. "Gorgeous."

Then he presses a kiss to my neck. "Perfect."

CHAPTER 32
JON

It's unreal. We're in Paris, wandering hand in hand along the river. The air is warm, and the breeze is cool. I thought Cassie might jump out of the plane last night. It spooked her, fully realizing how well off I am. Once the shock of it faded, she flirted with me at dinner and slept soundly in my arms. This morning she joined me in the little shower, pressing her slick wet body against mine until we both fit. It was perfect.

She hasn't stopped smiling since we landed. We buy espresso and crepes with Nutella and bananas from a sidewalk vendor, watching as he expertly spreads the batter over the round griddle and manipulates it with a large flat spatula. We nibble the warm hazelnut chocolate as we walk, taking in the sights and sounds of Paris. Cassie's eyes are wide, drinking in the color and light. As we pass, she greedily breathes in the smells of the string of cafes just opening for breakfast. She looks so happy I almost don't want to risk it. She might say no. It's probably too soon, but I don't care. I can't wait another day to ask her.

We pass Notre Dame, and I lead her toward the little bridge. As we cross, she glances at the railings covered with padlocks. She stops, looks down, and lifts one. "What's all this?"

I walk over, lean my hip against the rail and explain. "It's a love lock. For each lock on this bridge, a couple put their names on the lock and pledged their undying love to each other. They snap it on the bridge and throw the keys over the edge into the water below. It's a symbol of their everlasting love."

She adores the story. Her face lights up, and she bends to study the names. When she stands, she looks up at me with those big brown eyes. "That's incredibly romantic."

I put my hand in my pocket and fish out the golden lock, keys still attached and lift it so she can see. Her mouth opens into a little O as she studies the lock in my palm. I had it engraved with our names.

"Really?" she asks shyly, her full lips pressing into a thin line. "You want to do it?"

"You're my forever, Cass. I've known that for a long time. I'm sorry it took me so long to—"

She doesn't let me finish. Her arms are around my neck, and she's kissing me. When she finally pulls away, she takes the lock, and we pick a spot on the railing. Together we snap it closed and toss the key into the dark water below.

Cassie's eyes fill with affection. She rises on her toes at the same time as I drop to one knee. She pauses, not getting it at first. The people around us do, though, and they stop to watch.

I pull the ring out of my other pocket and hold it up to her. Her eyes widen, and she covers her mouth with her hands. "Cassie Hale, I've loved you from the moment I met you. You shared your heart with me, and now I'm asking if you'll share your life with me. I love you, baby. I always will. Cassie, will you marry me?"

My stomach twists as she stands there, frozen. The ring gets heavier as panic floods through me. It was too fucking soon. I shouldn't have asked her, but I had to know. I want it to be more. I want her forever.

My gaze drops and the ring feels heavy to hold without hope. Just before it passes my eyes, she's there, kneeling in front of me. There are tears on her face, and she's smiling. "You can't take that away yet. I didn't give you my answer."

"It's okay, Cass. I was greedy. I shouldn't have pushed you. I should have—"

She grabs my shoulders and shakes me hard. "Yes, you should have! Yes, I want to marry you!" She tips her head to catch my eyes. "Yes to everything."

My chest fills with too many emotions all at once. I think I'm going to burst apart. I slip the ring on her finger, and Cassie throws her arms back around my neck. We're kneeling next to a fence panel of locks on the Pont des Arts Bridge, eye-to-eye, nose-to-nose, and she leans in to kiss me.

It's not a regular, careful Cassie kiss. It's hot lips, desire, and hope mingling together and flowing through us both. That wasn't bullshit before. It wasn't showmanship. She's told me so much, opened up the most private parts of her existence to me.

She's my other half, and I know it.

There's no one else like Cassie Hale, and there never will be.

AUTHOR'S NOTE

In mid-2015, Paris said *au revoir* to love locks. Their Pont Des Arts Bridge swooned hard under the weight of over one million padlocks—the equivalent of over forty elephants—with parts of the bridge collapsing into the Seine River. Parisian city workers removed the locks to preserve the integrity of the structure and ensure the historic landmark remains safe for visitors. Still, the experience of standing on that bridge, witness to the love of the many couples who left a lock and threw away the keys, was sublime. It's an example of real-life romance I wanted to preserve in these pages and share with you, so that even if you didn't have the chance to visit in person, you can still experience it within this book.

*****

Now for a more difficult subject. Every year countless women are plagued by pelvic pain with no idea what to do about it. Most suffer in silence, unaware it's a condition they can manage with help from a medical professional.

Sometimes conditions flare up from abuse, other times it's from a difficult pregnancy or surgery. No one talks about it, so very few people know it's a thing, a real problem that makes life so much harder than it has to be.

It took me nearly three years to cross paths with a women's health physical therapist. She saved me. At the time, I was recovering from a very difficult pregnancy, but I'd experienced underlying issues with sex and pain my entire life. It wasn't until I started writing that I realized my descriptions of sexual sensations confused my editor. She circled the word 'sharp' and questioned it in the margin. It was the first time someone suggested that sex isn't supposed to hurt. I've since learned that women with this condition often describe sex that way. It's not pleasant, it's painful, and the only way to manage a relationship is to learn to love pain. It's that or nothing—or so I'd always thought.

It's taken years to undo the damage my seriously fat babies, surgeries, and bad habits caused, but I'm getting there. I wanted to draw attention to this matter because it affects so many women and they suffer alone when they don't need to.

Women's health physical therapists often work in conjunction with an OB/GYN. There aren't many of them in the US, but they do exist and, if you have this condition, it's worth the time and expense to visit one of them. Ask your doctor. Younger physicians are more likely to be aware of chronic pelvic pain issues and treat your request seriously.

If you'd like to read more about this topic, an excellent resource is *A Headache in the Pelvis*, a book by doctors David Wise and Rodney Anderson.

Sex doesn't have to hurt. There's hope.

READ MORE LARGE PRINT ROMANCE BY H.M. WARD NOW!

Turn the page to enjoy a free sample of *New York Times* bestselling novel

SCANDALOUS

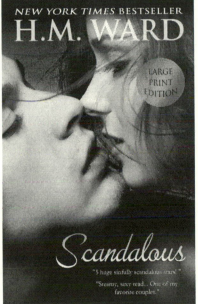

*****

Make sure you don't miss new releases!
Text HMWARD (one word) to 24587
to receive a text reminder on release day.

CHAPTER ONE

Rain splattered on the windshield of the cab in globs. Each splash sounded like a rock. I was used to nasty storms from living in Texas for so long, but it made the people who never left New York cringe. The cabbie was an oversized man with pasty skin and too much hair. He had a dark ball cap pulled down low, concealing his face. As we drove into the storm, he pushed his hat farther back, as if ball caps hindered vision. The man was leaning forward, practically pressing his face against the windshield.

We drove east in silence. He didn't try to make small talk, and I was glad about that.

This homecoming wasn't something I wanted to discuss. I still didn't want to be here, but there was nowhere left to go. The car pulled off the expressway, and after a few turns, the cab rolled down a narrow street in Port Jeff. Through the rain, porch lights blazed promising warmth inside the rows of homes.

"Here we are," the cabbie stated with complete indifference. As he told me the total, he wrote something on a clipboard, and tossed it back onto the front seat next to him.

Hesitating for a moment, I looked up at the brown brick facade and swallowed. Maybe this wasn't a good idea. I'd left Long Island over ten years ago, and, although I missed it, I had never wanted to come back. Yet, here I was.

The cabbie cleared his throat, waiting. I blinked once, pushing away the doubt that crawled up my spine, and dug into my purse. It pained me to hand him the last of my money, but I did. He grumbled something, expecting me to be cheap because I looked like a drowned rat, but I said, "Keep the change."

"Sure thing, Princess. I'll buy a new yacht to park next to the other one." The man laughed. He sounded like a llama choking on a shoe. Fine. It wasn't a big tip, but it was all I had. I got the clear impression he didn't think Little Miss Texas should be wandering around big bad New York, like some redneck yokel who just discovered shoes.

Ignoring him, I slid off the seat. Kicking open the door, rain splattered down and I was instantly wetter. I didn't think that was possible. I had one bag with me and two others in the trunk. Drops of freezing rain ran down my neck and into my coat making me shiver. I'd forgotten how different men acted here. They didn't hold doors or help girls with their bags. After I ran around to the back of the cab, I grabbed my suitcases and slammed the trunk shut.

As the red taillights faded into the darkness, the front door of 6A opened. A young woman with long dark hair ran down the porch stairs and straight at me. "Abby!" In two bounds she was across the puddles, hugging me like I'd never left.

"Hey, Kate," I hugged her back. She didn't seem to care that I was sopping wet, and now, so was she. Holding my shoulders in her hands, she examined me under the streetlight. Her eyes were still vibrant, and every ounce as green as I remembered.

"I can't believe it's been so long since I've seen you," Kate said grinning, shaking her head. "I have no idea why you ran away and failed to tell your best friend about it, but I would have traded anything to get to see you again. And now you're here!" She hugged me again. I wasn't much of a hugger, and neither was she, but she was right. With the way I'd left, I didn't expect such a warm reception. "Come on, let's go inside. I have a spiked hot cocoa with your name on it." She reached for my bags, and then made a beeline for the front door with me on her heels.

*****

Kate didn't know why I'd left, and I never told her. It was complicated. As I stepped over the threshold, I glanced around her apartment. It was warm and clean, decorated like an art gallery with beautiful artwork on the walls. The room was peaceful, painted with soft blues and browns—not like the girl with the bright orange bedroom she had when we were younger. Kate seemed to have gotten over her fascination with neon colors.

Pushing her dripping hair out of her face, Kate said, "Come on. I'll show you your room, and then we can catch up." Following Kate's path of puddles, I walked between the living room and kitchen to a back hallway. The apartment was larger than it appeared from the street. After passing a bathroom, I stopped in the doorway of a bedroom. Kate grabbed my bags from me, putting them under a window and throwing towels on the floor in front of them to soak up the water. "And this, Miss Abigail Tyndale, will be your residence for as long as you like."

"It'll only be a year, Kate. I'll go as soon as I can. I don't want to burden you." I felt horrible having to do this in the first place, and she was being so nice. Kate was the same selfless person from a decade ago. I bet she still dragged half dead cats off the street and took them to the vet, happily footing their medical bills and finding them a new home.

Kate folded her arms over her chest, and hung her head. "You're gonna run again, aren't you? First chance you get, you'll head for the hills and go back to no-mans land." It was a statement. An obvious observation. A dark tendril of hair clung to Kate's cheek, water dripping down her face like tears. Her green eyes were on me, wanting an answer.

No one willingly ran to no-mans land. I sure didn't and standing there with her, it felt like I'd never left. It felt like I had my best friend back, and I missed her. No one took her place in all the time I was gone. She was the kind of person who didn't say what you wanted to hear—she said what you needed to hear. Friends like her were rare.

I smiled at her, "This isn't my home anymore. I don't belong here." My moist clothing clung to me like wet toilet paper. I repressed a shiver. A hot shower really sounded divine.

"You belong with your family," she stated, stubbornly.

I wondered if she'd heard—if she knew. One night, several years ago, my parents were driving back from dinner and never got home. They were hit, head on, by a car going 90 miles per hour. Everything shattered. There was nothing left. No chance for survival. No chance to say good-bye. "They're all dead, Kate. I'm alone," I said softly staring at her.

She smiled sadly at me, "I know Abby, but that wasn't what I meant. Your friends are your family now. You're not alone, unless you choose to be." As she left my room, she said over her shoulder, "It's time to stop running."

CHAPTER TWO

The door clicked shut. There was truth in her words, truth that I didn't want to hear. After a hot shower, I donned a pair of sweats and headed out to the living room. The plastic soles of my slippers made me sound like a water buffalo traipsing through the apartment. The wooden floors didn't conceal much noise, although the dark wood looked nice.

Kate was in the kitchen, standing by the stove, with a kettle in her hand. She beamed when she saw me. "Choose your poison, cinnamon schnapps or something stronger?" Kate had changed her waterlogged clothing too and was wearing a pair of boxers and a tank top. Her damp hair was pulled back into a ponytail.

Sitting on the couch, I pulled my legs in tight. "No schnapps, Kate. Just plain cocoa."

She arched an eyebrow at me, the bottle pausing before she poured it into my cup. "Seriously? No alcohol?"

I nodded. "Part of the vows—alcohol is only used in rituals." If Kate's eyebrows climbed any higher, they'd be in her ponytail. I laughed, "I'm fine, Kate. It doesn't have to be spiked."

"It should be," she mumbled, carrying over two oversized cups. Handing me one, she sat down across from the sofa on a large suede chair. After taking a sip she asked, "So, this must be rough." I nodded once, not meeting her eyes. "How long were you working there?"

I sipped my drink, not looking up, "Since I started seminary, so twelve years or so." The mug felt warm against my hands. I wished she'd talk about something else, but my mind was drawing a blank. It was like I couldn't think of a single thing to derail her questions.

"What was your job?" she asked carefully.

"Preacher. Minister. The normal churchy kind of stuff." Taking another sip, I looked up at her. I knew what she wanted to ask me, but I didn't want to talk about it. Not yet, anyway.

Her legs were pulled sideways, mirroring mine. She was leaning on her left arm, steaming mug in her right hand. "That sounds nice." She was trying to be sweet. Nice was the last word for what it was. If Dante had a version of Hell with pictograms, I think the gun-wielding cow folk would have been around level four. At first I adored them, like crazy old coots, but the longer I was there the more I saw that they thought I was the nutty one. I nodded again. Kate looked at her mug and blurted out the dreaded question. "So what'd you do?"

Kate's green eyes were wide, a grin on her face. "I have to ask. It's killing me, Abby. For the past decade I'm lucky if I've heard from you twice. And then all of a sudden you get tossed on your ass—by a church! Did you curse them out from the pulpit? Or what?"

I cringed. "Maybe." She knew I had issues controlling my tongue. Before I headed south and signed on the clergy dotted line, I swore like a sailor. Spewing profanity from the pulpit was a normal occurrence for me, although the words they blanched at were words like 'crap' and 'hell.' Really, Hell is a noun. They should have gotten over that, but that wasn't what got me banished. I hedged, "Kate, I really don't want to rehash it. I did something bad—something that should have gotten me fired—but they said that they'd keep me if I took a mandatory sabbatical." There it was. The statement I practiced on the plane flying up here.

"So a year of vacation—that's not that bad, right?" she sipped from her mug, green eyes peering at me.

I laughed, trying to defuse the tension I felt building in my shoulders. I was mad, angry. This wasn't fair, but it's the way things were. I had to deal with it. I said, "If that's what they did, it would have been fine. But they didn't." I hesitated. Talking about this just made me more emotional. I walked into this mess. I brought it on myself and now I was homeless. I decided to tell her more. It was Kate, and I doubt she'd condemn me for what I did, although I wouldn't specify exactly what—not yet. "The church board said it was a year in the desert—they wouldn't pay my salary—and that if I wanted to remain employed, that I had to do this."

"So, basically you were tossed out on your ass with no money?" Kate's expression was surprised. "That doesn't sound like a churchy thing for them to do."

I nodded, "Yeah, but it's actually much worse." My stomach sank. This was the kicker and it was my own damn fault.

"How could it possibly be worse?" her jaw was hanging open, her mug tilted precariously to the side, its contents threatening to spill onto the floor. To Kate, bad was a finding a mugger in the bathroom stall, and what I was about to tell her would set her on full attack. I just hoped I wouldn't get blasted when I told her how stupid I was. This was the biggest mistake I ever made, aside from getting almost fired.

Avoiding her gaze, I explained, "They hired me while I was in college. I was working on a ministry degree and I could have been an assistant minster somewhere, maybe with youth or something. But this church wanted me as their one and only minister. They wanted me to do seminary. It was three years of grad work on top of the student loans I already had. I said I couldn't afford it, but we reached an agreement..."

Kate groaned, "Oh no. Tell me you didn't."

My throat tightened. I stared into my cocoa. I was stupid. While most kids had some debt from school that followed them around like a puppy, stealing their meager wages, making it harder to survive, I had a freaking walrus. It sat on me, it squashed me, and made my life a living hell. I thought Kate's parents were deranged lunatics. They were anti-credit card. I can't imagine the bitch-slap her mom would give me if I admitted to my walrus-sized loans.

Pressing my lips together, I nodded, "I did. I took out more loans to pay for grad school. The way my contract with the church was worded, it said that they would pay off my debt as part of my salary." It didn't seem like a bad idea at the time, and I really didn't know the difference between ten dollars and ten grand. Apparently the lenders know that stuff. So did the church board.

Kate closed her eyes, shaking her head, immediately catching on, "And since they aren't giving you a salary for this entire year..."

"I have to repay my astronomical student loans on my own." I ran my fingers through my hair, practically pulling it out. There were so many major mistakes, and they were all super-sized. "I don't know what to do, Kate. The church provided the parsonage. They gave me enough money to pay my bills and eat. It wasn't enough to save anything. I was lucky that I had enough money to get here. When I told them that, they said the lilies of the field don't worry about tomorrow and neither should I. What am I supposed to? If you hadn't taken me in, I'd have nowhere to go."

They screwed me. My church, the people I dedicated my life to, completely and totally screwed me. They wrote this off as a learning experience that would make me stronger. They broke their word about making sure my loans were paid every month without a second thought. Fury flamed to life inside of me. My fingers ran through my hair as that nauseating sense of desperation crawled up my throat again. It felt like I was being choked, but nothing was there. Hanging my head, I pressed my eyes closed, fighting to hold back the tears that were building behind my eyes.

Kate tapped the side of her cup, thinking, "Okay, let's not freak out, yet. We need to address the loans first. You have a place to stay and you don't have to worry about food, either." She grinned, "I'm an awesome cook. No more Spaghetti-os for you!" Glancing up at her, head in my hands, I couldn't find the smile within me. I felt crushed, like some huge ogre stepped on me, smashing me flat. "Okay, let's see. I didn't do the loan thing. My parents thought debt was the devil's doing. But loan companies have options in case of emergencies, deferments to make repayment easier if there's a crisis. Abby, have you filed for a deferment? I bet you could claim financial hardship and they'd give you a year or more before demanding another payment."

I shook my head, "I don't have anymore. We used them all."

"We?" she asked, her mouth gaping like a fish.

I cringed. It sounded utterly stupid now that I was explaining it to someone else. Sitting back in my chair, I looked up at her. "The board. They asked me to use all my deferments before they began repayment. I didn't think they'd toss me, so I used them... Oh my God, Kate." My eyes were wide. I didn't see how screwed I was until right then. Before saying it out loud, it had been an abstract thought of screwed-ness, drifting aimlessly through my mind. But now that I'd said it, it solidified and fell to my toes like a lead pancake.

SCANDALOUS

Kate leaned forward, putting her mug down, her game face on. "The past is the past, Abby. You can't change it. The only thing to do is try and come up with enough money to pay it. It can't be that much, right? What is it? A couple hundred bucks a month? That's doable. A minimum wage job would do that—you could work part-time and you'll be totally fine."

I shook my head and a tangle of reddish brown hair tumbled forward, freeing itself from my ponytail. "It's $3275 per month." I tucked the wayward strands behind my ear, saying the number completely numb. It was so astronomical that I should have been a doctor.

Kate's jaw dropped so wide that I could see every tooth in her head. "Holy fuck! How much do you owe?"

"Just over $270,000." Kate sat there stunned, recognizing the walrus. I sat there like the dumbass that I was, shaking my head, pressing my fingertips to my temples. "I need a job. I need a good job, fast." If I kept saying it, maybe I wouldn't freak out.

Kate came to her senses. She blinked those bright green eyes, as she shook the shock away, "Abby, what's mine is yours. I'll help you as much as I can. Don't worry about rent or groceries. I'll take care of that for a while." She shook her head, "Damn, that's a lot of debt. You need to make at least four grand or you won't have enough money after taxes. The market sucks here right now. And your degree doesn't help you."

"I know. I tried to find work in Texas, before I left, but even down in God's country I'm useless. No one wants a minister around when they aren't at church." They told me some crap about not wanting God looking over their shoulders at work. That stuff was for Sunday, as if they could lock God in the church building.

Kate frowned, "What else have you done since high school?" I didn't answer. My brain reached back trying to think of something unrelated to my ministry degrees. Kate straightened in her seat, an idea spreading across her face, "Ooh! What about art? Tell me you took some college art classes." Before I could answer she bounded down the hallway and came back holding a newspaper. She flicked through the pages.

"Yeah," I said slowly, watching her flip through the thin newsprint, "I took some art history, photography, and a painting class—but they were all electives with an emphasis on religious art."

She snorted, "Of course they were," she glared at me from over the top of the paper, "but you aren't going to tell anyone else that, unless they ask. Got it? Besides, most early art was religious anyway. It won't matter."

"Kate," I began to protest, but stopped when she slammed the paper down in front of me. Her narrow finger pointed toward an article that said:

LOCAL MUSEUM OPENS SOON.

I stared at the paper, but couldn't fathom what she was suggesting. "Clue me in, Kate. What are you thinking?"

"Well, a few weeks ago someone called MOMA looking for a new curator, and it was this place!" She pointed to the paper again. "I was the one who took the call. Abby, they're brand new, so they can't afford a seasoned professional—they need someone like you. Odds are it'll pay your loans and maybe give you a little pocket change. In other words, it's a crap job that no one can live off of unless they have an awesome roommate like me!" She beamed. "Plus, a reference from MOMA can't hurt. I'll call her first thing tomorrow." For the first time in days, I smiled and laughed. Maybe things would work out after all.

CHAPTER THREE

Or maybe not.

My heart sank, clunking into the bottom of my shoes as the dreaded words poured out of the woman's mouth, "The position has been filled." The girl at the desk informed me before I even finished saying my name. The vastness of the empty room seemed to make her voice louder. "It was earlier today, actually. I'm sorry, dear. I tried to get hold of you, but there was no cell number."

My shoulders slumped slightly, though I tried to hide it. Kate had spent the morning on the phone to get me this interview. There was no way I could afford a cell phone, so I didn't have one. Apparently Kate's recommendation wasn't enough to overcome the preacher thing. I smiled softly at her, "Thank you for trying. I really appreciate it."

As I turned to leave, she called out, "Hon!" I stopped and turned back to face her. She was scrawling something on a notepad. The museum was closed, so she was wearing jeans and a tee shirt. Plaster was splattered across her lap. "Wait!" I stopped, as she crossed the room quickly. "Listen, I heard that the Galleria needs help. It's not a museum, but it's an art job.

"The Galleria?" I asked, looking at the paper she handed me.

"Yeah, it's not too far from here. It's on the south shore in the Hamptons. Some rich guy owns it. That job will get snapped up fast. If I were you, I'd head over there right now." She smiled at me. Her kindness floored me. I stood there for a moment before I found my voice.

SCANDALOUS

"Thank you. Thank you so much!" I looked at the address as I slipped back inside Kate's car. She worked at the Museum of Modern Art, otherwise known as MOMA, and said I could use her car. She worked crazy hours and said she wouldn't miss it.

The maps of Long Island that I had in my head were old, but I thought I knew where the address that the woman handed me was located. I didn't have a cell phone, and Kate's car was too old to have GPS. I looked at the address again, wondering if I should go—if I could pull off a job interview when I didn't even know what the job was. I was flying by the seat of my pants and hating every moment of it.

That choking sensation climbed out of my belly again, threatening my sanity. Without a job I'd lose everything I worked so hard on for the past ten years. My credit would be trashed, student loan collectors would harass me to no end, and my contract with the church would be violated.

I didn't think anything of it at the time, requiring a person to keep their credit in good standing seemed like a reasonable part of a job. However, since they were the ones that caused the financial distress, it hardly seemed fair now.

Glancing in the rearview mirror, I pulled out. How hard would it be to fake my way through an interview? Anyway, I was already dressed. No point in giving up, not yet. Where there's a will, there's a way—and other crap like that sputtered through my mind. What was the worst that could happen? Without hesitation, I drove directly to the address on the paper. My jaw nearly fell off my face when I pulled up. It was a large studio and art gallery—and it was beachfront property—on the most expensive part of Long Island. The official name was Jonathan Gray Fine Art & Galleria. It was in carved golden letters on a blue sign in front of the door.

Stepping from my car, I hurried up the front walk, noticing the white sand. The sound of the ocean crashing into the shore filled my ears. When I pulled open the door, several women dressed far better than me sat waiting in a posh lobby. Confidently, I walked to the desk, although I felt lacking when I saw the other women's clothing. Their skirts and blouses hugged their bodies as if the garments were custom made. I was wearing my Texas Target dress with a white collared shirt underneath. Holy crap. I looked like a Sunday School teacher, or a nun in her street clothes. These were the wrong clothes for a place like this, but it was too late to do anything about it now.

The receptionist smiled wanly at me and handed me a clipboard. "You're late," she scolded. "I shouldn't even let you in, but since they haven't started the first round yet, I'll make an exception. Fill out your paperwork quickly. Mr. Gray doesn't have all day."

I nodded, smiling, and sat down next to a breathing Barbie doll. She arched a perfectly plucked brow at me, no doubt questioning my black frock and clunky shoes. Ignoring her, I filled out my paperwork. My heart raced a little bit. I didn't realize how much I wanted this, but I did. I missed doing creative things; I missed the challenge of it. And the job description plastered across the top of the papers made me giddy. I would be a gallery assistant. The salary was stated with an additional commission on each sale. I'd easily be able to pay my loans on time, and not mooch off of Kate. Hope swelled in my chest.

It took two hours for them to call my name. I was the last candidate. I followed the receptionist into a large room. There were several floor-to-ceiling windows that overlooked the ocean. My eyes went straight to the windows, staring at the sea. I didn't realize how much I missed it.

"Miss Tyndale," a man's voice called me back to reality. He held out a chair for me before moving around the long empty table to the other side. "I'm Gus Peck. I'll be conducting your interview. As you know we are a prestigious art studio. Jonathan Gray's works sell for a premium to affluent clientele. Are you comfortable working with the wealthy?"

Smiling, I leaned forward, "Yes. I've worked with many different people in the past. Some were difficult, but that was only because they demanded the best. Other personalities may have seemed easier to deal with at first, but they proved harder to assist." Was that a good answer? Interviewing for church jobs was very different. There was a fine line between telling them what they wanted to hear and what I really thought. Everyone was on best behavior, asking questions that usually didn't matter, but Gus' question seemed rather practical. It threw my footing off a little bit, as did his reply.

"How's that?" Gus asked, jotting down things on a yellow notepad as I spoke, his eyes not lifting to meet mine.

How is that, Abby? I was totally making stuff up, pulling answers out of the air on the fly. Explaining my rationale, I replied, "Well, the difficult people came across that way because they were demanding, but demanding people know what they want. They have clear expectations and expect them to be met." Gus stopped scribbling and looked up at me as I continued, "It can be intimidating if you haven't dealt with them before. But the easy-going people are actually harder to help, because they usually don't know what they need. It takes more patience and time to assist them." My back was straight and I noticed that I was sitting on the edge of my seat. I tried to relax a little, to appear more confident. I wanted this job so much. It would fix everything. I smiled softly, noticing my accent seemed fuddled. I didn't sound like a New Yorker anymore, but I didn't sound Texan either.

Gus nodded, "Hmm. Interesting observation." I looked at him, slightly intimidated. The man was in his early thirties, blonde hair and blue eyes. He looked like a cover model for GQ, holding my application in his hands. His eyes scanned it again. When he was done, he looked over the top of my papers and pointed his pen at me, "You get points for not giving cookie-cutter answers, Miss Tyndale, but you have no previous sales experience. It says here that you were a minister... in Texas?" The man looked at me like I was insane. As soon as I answered that question, this job interview was over.

Before I could speak a voice came from the shadows at the end of the room. "So, that's where you went? Texas." That voice. It made my stomach flip. My body was instantly covered in goose bumps, every hair standing on end. Something inside my chest ached when he spoke. Although I hadn't heard it in years, I recognized his warm playful tone instantly. I'd know him anywhere.

My pulse quickened and I suddenly felt much more nervous than I had a moment ago. Jaw hanging open, I turned and stared at him like he was a ghost. "Jack?"

*****

~Order the large print edition of SCANDALOUS now from Amazon or Barnes & Noble~

MORE FERRO FAMILY BOOKS

TRYSTAN SCOTT
~BROKEN PROMISES~
******

JONATHAN FERRO
~STRIPPED~
******

NICK FERRO
~THE WEDDING CONTRACT~
*****

BRYAN FERRO
~THE PROPOSITION~
*****

SEAN FERRO
~THE ARRANGEMENT~
******

PETER FERRO GRANZ
~DAMAGED~
******

MORE ROMANCE BY H.M. WARD

SCANDALOUS

SCANDALOUS 2

SECRETS

THE SECRET LIFE OF TRYSTAN SCOTT

DEMON KISSED

CHRISTMAS KISSES

OVER YOU

HOT GUY

And more.

To see a full book list, please visit:
http://www.hmward.com/pages/books.htm

CAN'T WAIT FOR H.M. WARD'S NEXT STEAMY BOOK?

Let her know by leaving stars and telling her what you liked about

STRIPPED 2

in a review!

ABOUT THE AUTHOR
H.M. WARD

New York Times bestselling author HM Ward continues to reign as the queen of independent publishing. She is swiftly approaching 13 MILLION copies sold, placing her among the literary titans. Articles pertaining to Ward's success have appeared in The New York Times, USA Today, and Forbes to name a few. This native New Yorker resides in Texas with her family, where she enjoys working on her next book.

You can interact with this bestselling author at:
Twitter: @HMWard
Facebook: AuthorHMWard
Webpage: www.hmward.com

Made in the USA
Lexington, KY
25 May 2019